THE REAL LONG JOHN SILVER
AND OTHER PLAYS

THE REAL
LONG JOHN SILVER
and other plays
Barnes' People III

PETER BARNES

faber and faber
LONDON · BOSTON

First published in 1986 by
Faber and Faber Limited
3 Queen Square London WC1N 3AU

Phototypeset by Wilmaset, Birkenhead, Wirral
Printed in Great Britain by
Redwood Burn Ltd, Trowbridge, Wiltshire
All rights reserved

All rights whatsoever in these plays are strictly reserved
and applications for permission to perform them, etc. must be
made in advance, before rehearsals begin,
to Margaret Ramsay Ltd, 14a Goodwins Court,
St Martins Lane, London WC2N 4LL

Lines from the song 'Unforgettable' by Irving Gordon are
reproduced by kind permission of Bourne Inc., Bourne Music
Ltd and Bourne Co., New York, copyright 1951.
Lines from 'Put It There, Pal', written by Johnny Burke and
composed by Jimmy Van Heusen, are reproduced by kind
permission of Chappell-Morris Ltd, London,
and Bourne Co., New York, copyright 1945.

British Library Cataloguing in Publication Data

Barnes, Peter, *1931–*
    The real Long John Silver : and other plays.
    I. Title
    822'.914   PR6052.A668
    ISBN 0–571–14558–2

Library of Congress Cataloging-in-Publication Data

Barnes, Peter, 1931–
    The real John Silver and other plays.
    I. Title.
    PR6052.A668R39   1986   822'.914   86–11641
    ISBN 0–571–14558–2 (pbk.)

CONTENTS

INTRODUCTION

A torch-bearing crowd arrived in front of the house of the great French opera singer Nourrit to give him an ovation after a performance. But he thought they had come to mock him because he knew he had not been in good voice that night. In his despair he jumped out of the window and killed himself. Most times I understand him only too well, but with the short plays I have not yet felt the urge to jump.

This is the third and last of the series which began with *Barnes' People I* continued with *Barnes' People II* and now ends with *Barnes' People III*.

In a sense they are all true stories, only the names have been changed to protect the guilty. Though set in different times and places, they celebrate the particularity of individuals, each of whom has a distinctiveness which makes them that which they are and no other. Kant kept his socks up with a device operated from his top pocket and Wordsworth opened his letters with a dirty jam knife. Such individuality, visible yet unknowable, is a defence against cruelty which feeds on complacency and indifference.

I do not write about ordinary men and women. The variety and enormity of the world and its people and their infinite possibilities make belief in the ordinariness of ordinary people a blasphemy. The earth contains multitudes of beings unique in their creative energy for good and evil. So many Trojan Helens called Ada, so many Leonardos called Fred. Genius is not the exception but the rule. But the radiant light lies shuttered by fear, helplessness and the wicked triviality of day to day living. It is plain we have always needed another, better, social system to let it all shine out.

The great sin is the complete lack of compassionate vision, the inability to conceive of life existing on any other level than our own limited experience of it. Not knowing or understanding, ice-picks are needed to break the frozen seas within. Yet mankind is more than crumbs of dust at best and dirt-balls at worst.

Perhaps that is why I often think of Robert Damies and smile despite myself. Damies tried to kill Louis XV with a penknife. Sentenced to have his right hand burnt off and then boiling pitch poured into his wounds and after that to be torn apart by horses, he commented, 'It's going to be a hard day.'

It seems perverse to be even slightly optimistic when everything points to the final sunset. Yet even that prospect need not be totally black if we remember that the entire nuclear apparatus is dependent on communications and all communication is dependent on telephone lines and telephone lines usually go 'kaput' in heavy rain. So it is highly likely the heads of state will not get to their bunkers in time. Now, I submit, that alone is cause for a degree of optimism. Besides, all things living and dead finally become redundant so we can at least hope that men and women will, one day soon, be replaced by an entirely new species, eternal and sublime. An exhilarating thought for generations I'll never see – I should live that long.

PETER BARNES
1986

These plays were first broadcast on BBC Radio 3 in August 1986. The casts were as follows:

After the Funeral

HARRY	Sean Connery
TOM	Donald Pleasence
MAX	John Hurt

The Peace of Westphalia

HERZBRUDER	Bob Peck
JACOB	David Suchet
TERZKY	David Warner

The Real Long John Silver

HENRY	Ian Carmichael
MADGE	Anna Massey
GEORGE	Paul Eddington

The Heirs of Diogenes

DIOGENES	Michael Hordern
CRATES	Mike Gwilym
ALEXANDER	Simon Callow

Sisters

IRENE	Wendy Hiller
BARBARA	Ann Todd
KATHERINE	Renée Asherson

Dancing

SUSAN	Angela Pleasence
PAULLEIN	Michael Maloney
DIANE	Sian Phillips

xi

The Perfect Pair

BURKE	Norman Rodway
HARE	Gerald Murphy
DR KNOX	Alan Howard

The Three Visions

BARNES	Robert Stephens
YOUNG MAN	Anton Lesser
OLD MAN	Lionel Jeffries

All eight plays were produced by Ian Cotterell.

AFTER THE FUNERAL

A room. Three men seated at a table drinking.

HARRY: Too late for words, too late for tears. Why doesn't
anybody get out of life alive? She isn't living and why not? If
I had the power to make her I would, I would. If I'd been
with her then, 2.23 British Mean Time, I'd've caught her
spirit as it left her body. But I wasn't there, turned away for a
second and her last heartbeat had gone. Missed my chance of
having her with me always. I'm a poor dumb brute, a swirl of
quirks, a tap-dancing ghost and she was jealous if the
sunlight touched me, oh yes, oh yes. Our love caused
earthquakes in Panama and beyond. Others were covered
with hatred like horse mange but Anna was never corrupted.
Now she rots under marble. What am I going to do now? Do
now? I come back home and the house is empty; she's not
here and the days are blank. Fifteen years together . . .

TOM: Here, you'd better have another drink, these're bad times
for you, Harry. You're old when you're my age so I can tell
you, Anna was the best. We all know how hard this life is on
the nerves but she never complained. I used to hold her up as
an example to Betsy. You know I was with Betsy all those
years because I couldn't stand Sundays alone. But she was
difficult. They all are. But Anna always had the right word
for the occasion. One time Betsy went on about wanting to
hear the patter of tiny feet. Anna told her to rent some mice.

MAX: She was like a mother to my three girls. They're more
difficult when they're young. They want to be happy, so
they're taken in by feelings. They would never've got started
right without Anna. She worried about the way they were so
loose with money. The most important thing for them is
spending the stuff. I tried to argue with them with the back
of my hand but Anna said that wasn't the way. She talked to
them; she had brains behind the paint; she'd done the
rounds, that little lady. How old was she, thirty-three?

3

TOM: My mother died when she was thirty-three. I remember
coming home from school one day and she was missing.
The woman next door said she'd gone to the ice-house –
that's what we called the isolation hospital. I never saw her
again. I didn't go to visit her 'cause I never liked hospitals
and anyway, I didn't especially *feel* like seeing her. Funny
your Anna dying the same age as my mother.

HARRY: She didn't. Anna was forty-nine.

MAX: It does her credit, she certainly knew how to hide her age.

TOM: She could've prolonged her working life years – if she
hadn't died.

HARRY: She was RC, you know. Incense, wafers, being led by
unmarried men in black dresses sitting in boxes listening to
other people's secrets, believing wine can be turned into
blood and bread into flesh. Anna believed them for her sake
and resisted them for mine. She must've heard thousands of
sermons against sin and she stood firm. She was flint-souled
against all the pleas and prayers.

TOM: Virtue's too icy-cold for me. In this world you've got to
keep your tootsies warm. You can have all your
Holy-Rollers. As long as I empty my bowels regular of a
morning, I'm fine.

HARRY: One good thing, the dead don't hear church bells. It
was a brutal business all round. Anna used to come away
from those church sessions dripping with sweat. I think
they had something to do with her dying. They cost her,
but she paid. She said she'd suffer Hell for my sake and
now she's gone – not to Hell, not Anna, too dark there for
Anna; she liked bright lights and warm beds.

TOM: Her stockings were never crumpled and her get-up-and-go
never got up and went. What did she die of, Harry?

HARRY: Booze. Doc Bellows said if she'd drunk water she'd've
lived till Judgement Day. But who wants to live that long?
She took the cure but all she got was a skin as hard as
crab-apples. Aside from that she was fine, if you don't
count her teeth – they dropped out two years ago. It meant
more meat for me but it was unpleasant for her.

4

MAX: It just shows a woman doesn't have to be beautiful to be
   successful.

HARRY: She had an inner beauty. Other people saw it too.
   That's why clients came miles. God knows how many cheap
   Awayday tickets she must've sold for British Rail.

TOM: When you're young, good looks're everything. Later, you
   need something else to make your mark. Anna had class;
   sometimes she was almost regal.

HARRY: That's why she was known as the Queen of the East
   Acton Red Light District.

TOM: And she knew just how tough our job is. Most people
   think pimping is an easy touch.

MAX: How can it be easy? We're on the go twenty-four hours a
   day. We're bodyguards, father confessors, husbands,
   lovers, agents. It never stops. A contented man sleeps
   contented but I lay awake nights wondering what new
   regulations the Vice Squad's coming up with. All
   middle-class reform does is drive up the price of whoring so
   the working class can't afford it. It's just one problem after
   another. The work involved marketing one successful
   prostitute is immense. I should know, I used to be in
   advertising.

TOM: When I first got started as a pimping back-door man it
   was easier. I must've told you before I was selling
   newspapers when Lilly Tibbet asked me to hand out her
   calling cards – 'Wham Bam Thank You, Ma'am' – to any
   likely looking customers. She gave me a percentage of
   money earned from 'em. We got pally and I moved in as a
   chilli pimp. Lilly had friends and pretty soon I was running
   an eight-girl stable. I'd zazzle each of 'em twice a month
   and beat 'em up maybe every three to show I was still
   interested. That's all they expected.

MAX: It's different now, Tom. I have to be tromboning every
   night of the week and I'm only stabling three.

TOM: When I was an ace, pimping was more of a cottage
   industry. We had time to enjoy the good things of life. I
   used to like dressing well in silk shirts, cravat, tie-pin, I was

5

togged to the bricks. Now I go around all day in floppy carpet slippers. There was money to be made, of course. But most of it vanished quicker than the pimps of yesterday – Six-rings Charlie, Bosco Canns, Alhambra Jack Brody, Jersey Merton. Names, Max, names! They *were* pimping. Where are they now? Dope got Al Rush and Sneed Ern; King Cress left town with a knife in his back and Gus Moranty and Cairo George were all jailed, all clapped out, all bets off. I was careful when I was on the sunny side of Sugar Hill. I didn't dope, drink or gamble. So I'm more or less intact.

MAX: That side of poncing's got better, less sporty. It's a business like any other and it's best run by businessmen. The girls've got much worse though. No sense of responsibility. I've never seen a flatbacker pick up a book, for example. I've told them, books can teach you what to do and what not to say. I learnt from books you can be a ponce, prostitute or journalist, only don't talk like one. You can do anything as long as you don't give yourself away. But nobody listens. I've given up on them. Nowadays, they're too lazy to even talk in their sleep.

TOM: It was always hard to get them off their behinds and on to their backs.

HARRY: Anna was never like that. She was a worker. That's how we met. I was taking a busman's holiday in Morocco, looking at the brothels, seeing if I could pick up any tips. They had a big reputation at the time. I went to Little Mama's in Casablanca. You'd've been impressed, Max. They used a voucher system. A client would buy a voucher from Little Mama, go upstairs with a flatbacker of his choice and pay her with the vouchers. The girls never saw money. Anna was the star; did she work! Fifteen hours a day, seven clients an hour, one every four minutes. She hardly left her room. Sometimes she was on her back till four in the morning: a two-hundred-voucher-a-day girl was Anna. That didn't mean two hundred clients. Oh no, no, no. One man would buy four or five tickets like me. That's how I managed to talk to her. I found out she was British and homesick. But she couldn't get free. Little Mama worked closely with the police like all madames. I remember looking at Anna and deciding there and then to help. You could call me a romantic, I suppose. 'You want out? I'll get you out.' I felt like one of those knights in shining pants, rescuing a maiden from the dragon. Anna didn't believe me at first but I grabbed her hand and took her downstairs with me. I told Little Mama straight, Anna was coming home with me. We were both British – and proud of it. The old lady laughed, she wasn't going to let her best worker go just like that; she'd call the police. So I shot off her left kneecap. I was younger then. As she lay bleeding and moaning on the floor I told her if she tried to stop us, friends of mine would come and finish the job. Anna and me left hand in hand. I never regretted it. What started in blood, ended in roses.

TOM: I never heard that story before, Harry.

HARRY: It's why *Casablanca* was always our favourite movie. Memories, memories.

MAX: It shows we're as sentimental as the next man yet ponces always get a bad press. It's unfair! Girls without pimps are in deep holes open to all kinds of abuse; they can even be raped without being paid. We're not do-gooders but we do good: we help regulate a violent profession.

TOM: Bananas – I never cared about that. So long as I ate well, drank well, slept warm and dry and had money in my pocket and in my bank I was doing a hundred, happy as a sandboy.

MAX: I never wanted to be happy, just rich and powerful – which is the same thing I suppose.

HARRY: Happy? Don't talk to me about happy, that's buried out in marble town with her. What am I going to do now? I look around and I'm alone. Have you noticed the poor don't walk like other people? They go hunched, zig-zaggy against the wind. It's time to retire or get lost.

TOM: I'm the creaker not you, Harry. I was sixty-nine when I
    retired. I'd had a good innings but I knew I couldn't keep it
    up any more. But you've got years yet. You've taken a bad
    fall but the trick is to get mounted again, and quick.

HARRY: What're you saying? We've just had a cold meat party
    for Anna, she's lying out there all last debts paid.

MAX: You shouldn't be idle, Harry. It's the worst thing for you
    right now. You've got to be occupied.

HARRY: I haven't the heart for it.

TOM: The heart isn't involved.

HARRY: I couldn't face starting up all over again.

TOM: I wish I had the chance. Ahhh, the spring promise of it
    all.

HARRY: You know the work involved bringing an unknown
    flatbacker up to standard. Most don't know the basics of
    good whoring: clean linen and clean orifices – that's what
    we're selling. After all, I have a certain reputation. Anna
    and I were respected throughout British vice. Our names
    were synonymous with quality whoring. That didn't
    happen overnight. How can I take some green kitten and
    make her into another First Lady of Brotheldom?

TOM: I'm sure you wouldn't have to do the full Pygmalion bit,
    Harry.

HARRY: But I would. All three of us are up-market, flesh
    pedlars. We know clients aren't just paying for sex. They're
    shelling out for companionship, someone to listen to them
    and maybe just to be seen with a well-dressed woman. I'd
    have to show her how to dress properly, the right bars, the
    right conversation.

MAX: It's a challenge, Harry. The girl would have to be a free
    floater, of course – can't have her attached to a pimp or
    madame.

HARRY: If they're any good they wouldn't be allowed to float
    free. Besides, I'm no young flesh ace any more and who'd
    want a relic like me?

MAX: Come, come Harry. No false modesty. You're an
    institution. We've all learned from you. When I first came

into the profession you told me a whore's only as good as
her pimp. Words of wisdom, Harry. Your kind of expertise
can't be bought. You'll be snapped up once they know
you're back on the market.

TOM: What floating bantams have you got for us, Max?

MAX: (*Consulting a notebook*) Let's see what's in my little red
book. I know men who'd give thousands to get just a peep
at this . . . Ahh, now . . . Rosey Banks . . . no, no, she's
gone in the head . . . Ingrid Rogers . . . Yes, Ingrid's a
possible hit . . . Twenty-four, five feet nine, good breasts
and teeth. Blonde Swedish type, clean, quick, efficient.

TOM: Sounds good.

MAX: But limited. Too clinical for English tastes. Not flexible
enough to earn big. She plays the Ice Goddess well but
finds it difficult to adjust to other roles.

HARRY: That's essential. A whore has to be all things to all
men. And if she's a good actress she can keep her integrity
intact: she isn't doing anything, it's the other she.
Remember how good Anna was? One of her best clients
liked to set up a table in his bedroom to look like the Last
Supper and she'd come as Mary Magdalene with veil and
sandals. Another time she'd have to lie in a coffin and play
dead. That took talent for someone as alive as Anna. If
she'd wanted she could've been another Sybil Thorndyke or
worse.

MAX: Cross off Swedish Ingrid . . . Daisy Lucknow's a trim
chimer . . . and she's free . . .

HARRY: With everybody. She'd give it away to every beggar
with a hard story. Salt of the earth as a person but a disaster
as a business proposition.

MAX: Big Clair O'Hara's floating – all eighteen stone of her.
She's too much for you to carry at this time, Harry – no
offence . . . Ahh, I have it, that and them . . . The best
trim zazzler now at large . . . Rita Grass.

TOM: That's better. Rita has real potential; she's big booty.
She'll never have trouble breaking luck.

MAX: Twenty-three, five feet five, brunette, all roll and go. And

flexible. Her father used to be a contortionist for
Chipperfield. Circus love's her speciality.

HARRY: Isn't she macking with Sweet Sam Wilson?

MAX: Didn't you hear Sam came down with a fatal case of
death?

HARRY: Never thought he'd be that considerate.

MAX: He refused to pay a gambling debt. First man I ever saw
flattened by a steam-roller.

TOM: Sam and me had a sneering acquaintance but I didn't
know him.

HARRY: Not to know him was the best. Extortionist, thief,
impostor, liar, slanderer – he was a man with a completely
blemished record – so crooked he'd steal two left shoes.

MAX: A smile like concentrated vodka.

HARRY: A gorilla pimp of the old school. The business is better
off without the likes of Sweet Sam.

MAX: That's what Rita thought in the end. She was always
telling Sam to be more like you. She'd jump at the chance of
going into partnership. It'd be a big step up in class for her.

HARRY: What about me?

TOM: Harry, just talk to her. It's hard not working if you've
worked all your life. Suddenly you're redundant, not
wanted, not of use and the long days are longer and the
nights: I know.

MAX: It's business, Harry, and in business if you stand still, you
die. Just ring the girl, you don't have to commit yourself.
But she's an earner.

HARRY: No. In this life all relationships don't have to be based
on money. Because Anna isn't earning any more doesn't
mean she has no meaning for me. She does; she does. All
the years we were together I never went catting. No need,
she never lost her zazzle for me. It was reckless eyeballing
from the first moment we met, she always made my love
come down. Now she's thrust her final thrust, my mind's in
mud just thinking about a replacement. Why is life so sad?
Gentlemen, there's no question, like her, I shall be sleeping
alone tonight. It's a matter of honour – for my love's sake

   . . . You can ring Rita first thing tomorrow, Max. I'm sure
   it's what Anna would've wanted.

TOM: Delicately done, Harry.

MAX: It is indeed.

HARRY: Gentlemen, a toast . . . Anna . . . Unforgettable.

TOM ⎫
MAX ⎬ : Anna . . . (*They drink and then sing softly:*)
HARRY ⎭   'Unforgettable, that's what you are.
       Unforgettable, tho' near or far.
       Like a song of love that clings to me,
       How the thought of you does things to me.
       Never before has someone been more
       Unforgettable in every way,
       And for evermore that's how you'll stay.
       That's why, darling, it's incredible,
       That someone so unforgettable,
       Thinks that I am unforgettable too.

THE PEACE OF WESTPHALIA

A single pistol shot. Lights up on a clearing outside Osnabruck,
Westphalia, 1645. JACOB *and* HERZBRUDER *confront* COUNT
TERZKY.

JACOB: Thhhaa ooowwhh yyyrrraaa! Iiiieeee uuuhh!

HERZBRUDER: In other words, in the name of rape, robbery
and murder, throw down your arms. Throw down, throw
down! You may be protected, flesh frozen iron-hard by
magic amulets, so you are invulnerable to sword thrusts and
lead bullets. But you're not to mine and my next is aimed
straight at your beating heart. If I miss, my partner Jacob
will split your head clean to your teeth. Throw down!
Throw down your sword – and your money!
(COUNT TERZKY *throws down his sword and a bag of money.*)
Good . . . Jacob, pick 'em up! . . . I never make the
mistake of aiming at a man's head, skulls're too thick in
Germany, our bullets too soft. They have even less chance
to penetrate Germanic skulls than good ideas. Yours must
be metres thick wandering alone outside Osnabruck. Don't
you know this is killer country? A wasteland haunted by
thieves like Jacob and me. In the hard winter of '34 eating
men was in fashion hereabouts, yet you go alone,
fur-gowned, leather-booted, silk ribbons in your hat. We've
been at war near thirty years and you've learned nothing.
You must be a man of titled parts. See the Elbe river
beyond those trees. It's clear now but come evening 'twill
be full of corpses bob, bob, bobbing along down river to
the sea. They'd sinned up river, broken the law, been
caught out alone, unprotected. This is the year of Our Lord
1645 and no one, not priests, captains, kings or emperors
go alone and survive.

TERZKY: I left Königsberg escorted by a detachment of the
Imperial Cavalry but those armoured oafs wandered off in
the morning mist foraging for food and booty and forgot

their orders to guard me. However, I have a safe conduct pass from the Emperor Frederick and General Wrangel.

JACOB: (*Laughing*) Arrrrrrh pppaapp tttaa thhhh tuuuu.

HERZBRUDER: (*Laughing*) Arse-paper. Jacob says 'tis arse-paper now. A good joke – almost. Sorry you don't understand Jacob, a man of infinite parts and pretty humour. He could've become a stand-up Merry Andrew, a Court Wit to kings if Hessian troops hadn't torn out his tongue. It makes it difficult for him to reach a wider audience.

JACOB: Thhhh oooo waaa uuuhh urrrt.

HERZBRUDER: That's true too. Those who want to understand him do. Our world's laid waste but manners aren't quite dead here in Westphalia though everything else is . . . This is my partner Jacob Gotz and I'm Karl Herzbruder today – tomorrow I may be Sernful von Christoff, captain, or Julius Zingreff, Rudolf Weckherlin, Johann Schottel, pickman, murderer, whoremaster.

TERZKY: Count Christian Terzky of Bohemia where the lunatics come from. Once honoured confidant of the late Count Wallenstein, now adviser to the Emperor Frederick. I am also founder member of the famous literary institution, The Fruit Bearing Society under the patronage of Prince Ludwig of Anhalt-Köthen.

HERZBRUDER: We have a man of letters in our net.

JACOB: Wwrrriii eee daagerous fuuu oooff luuizzz Iiii oooleee tttruuu spoookk wooodddd.

HERZBRUDER: Jacob says writing is dangerous – full of lies.

TERZKY: Everything is.

HERZBRUDER: He only trusts the spoken word . . . What are we going to do with you, Count? We'll strip you jack-naked sure, but do we strip you as an alive or dead one?

JACOB: Deee eeezz eeeessuu.

HERZBRUDER: Yes, dead is easier, always.

TERZKY: These safe conduct passes mean nothing?

JACOB: Llleee thaaa nooo.

HERZBRUDER: Jacob says less than nothing. We'd slit you up now but we're eager for fresh talk – talk. So talk.

TERZKY: You know just how to put a guest at his ease. I'll be
able to talk easy knowing I can be pistolled, piked or
razored dead at any moment.

HERZBRUDER: 'Tis what all men live with daily . . . Let's sit
awhile on this bank by the river. We can be men of leisure,
take time out of the task of staying alive to talk and listen. Tell
us of the dirt in high places, Count. Our ears flap to hear of
intrigue, gossip and scandal, the dark doings of the great
rulers who know which side their bread's buttered and who
always make certain sure their supply of butter never runs out
– Marshal Turenne, Count Trauttmansdorf, William of
Brandenburg, the Imperialist John de Werth, the Swede
Stalhaus, the Hessian St André – Who's in? Who's out? Who's
quick? Who's dead? Entertain us, Count.

TERZKY: Entertain you? Sometimes I'm hard put to it to
entertain a doubt.

HERZBRUDER: Talk as if your life depended on it, Count.
We're out of touch here in winter quarters. Summer's our
paid killing time when we join some army, Catholic or
Protestant or whatever, for battles, sieges, atrocities and the
like. Come winter, war games stop cold. The countryside's
picked clean for large scale looting and veterans like us set
up in private business. Even here more die from winter
starving than summer foes. We are consumed away 'less we
are right thrifty robbers . . . Ah, here's a pleasant spot . . .
We'll sit here, Master Count . . .

JACOB: Bbbeeeeaauuu . . .

HERZBRUDER: 'Tis beautiful the river and the wild plum trees
there on the other bank . . . smell the grass . . . Jews say
the righteous dance in Paradise . . .

JACOB: Bbbeeeeaauuu . . .

HERZBRUDER: But spring is dangerous. It makes a man relax;
he begins to think life is worth living and forget 'tis but a
great dung-hill on who's top sits the war god, Mars, and the
stench covers the whole wide globe. Envy, hate, cruelty,
pride, greed and the other fair vices aren't blown away by
light spring breezes. Men like Jacob and me've stayed alive

17

'cause we don't cling to life. We think o' ourselves as
already dead: so we seize the day and anything else that
isn't nailed down.

TERZKY: Few will reach old age and be able to sit in chimney
corners, roasting apples and telling tales.

HERZBRUDER: Tell us some now; entertain us with news, man,
news.

TERZKY: There are rats in Brunswick, massacres in Breisach,
grass in Stuttgart streets, starvation in Saxony where the
greatest delicacies are slug soup and roast joint of hedgehog:
yet still hunger looks out through a thousand eyes.

JACOB: Nooo neeeuuu.

HERZBRUDER: No, 'tisn't news. It's commonplace stuff. Gi' us
wonders.

TERZKY: Last summer, Signor Ghigi, the Papal Nuncio,
purchased Barbarossa's embalmed heart. He kept it in a
silver snuff box until he got so hungry he suddenly plucked
it out of its rich resting place and swallowed it whole,
saying, he'd never eaten the heart of a king before.

JACOB: Yuuum uumm mmuuu tttaaazzz ruuuulll.

HERZBRUDER: Yes, it must've tasted as royal jelly tastes. My
kind of food.

TERZKY: The Bishop of Wurzburg has had a hard case of
witch-fever. He was holding daily *autos-da-fé*, fifteen flamed
in a morning, till I told the victims to stop screaming they
were innocent – no use at all – and instead accuse the
Bishop himself of being a secret Satanist, Lucifer's
liege-man. The Bishop immediately lost his taste for
burning, his zeal died, the fires went out.

HERZBRUDER: I've roasted and basted a Bishop or two over
slow fires. They don't like it. No, no. It reminds 'em o'
Hell-fires they expect to come.

TERZKY: As for the high-table people, they've been doing what
all high-table do – getting and begetting more of the same.
William of Brandenburg is to be betrothed to Louise of
Orange. Simon Dach, the poet, has written a lucrative
poem – seven hundred verses at two thalers a verse – in the

bride's honour. It's in the manner of Horace – not the Latin Horace but Horace J. Stoffeldorffer the Third. 'Sweet Louise you are fairer far than any star. Beautiful, kind and virtuous you are. For this we praise God on high. When like an angel you fell from the sky . . .' The truth is, unfortunately, that when Louise fell she fell straight on her face. It looks like a bottle of warts. The bride has a large dowry and a larger mouth – every time she yawns, her ears disappear. Her complexion's a delicate seasick green. She's a woman men dream of in the dark – it's less painful than seeing her in the light.

HERZBRUDER: We've heard when she goes into a cornfield, she frights the crows so badly they bring back the corn they stole the year before.

JACOB: Sheeee aaa wrrrr aaaa laaa yeeaa aaapppzzz.

HERZBRUDER: (*Laughing*) That's a marvellous jest . . . yes, she *is* . . .

TERZKY: What's he say?

HERZBRUDER: That Louise . . . no, you wouldn't understand. It won't translate. It's a play on words.

TERZKY: Ahh . . . Pity, those jests're the best . . . The most important wonder of the winter months has been the meeting in Prague of the surviving great magis, wizards, alchemists, masters of astronomy and astrology, the Cabbala and Hermetic Arts, led by Longmontanus. 'Twas in honour of the late Rudolf II. It's said they summoned Tycho de Brahe, Kepler, Rabbi Loew and Dr Dee from beyond the grave to join their discussion groups but I don't believe that; not completely. However, they did issue a catalogue of some of their latest works. They've found ways of making matches that strike when wet; of doubling a man's strength without using carbine thistle which is forbidden and they've found a new powder, by which, on a dark night, a man can hear the softest sounds and whispers from a great distance off.

HERZBRUDER: That'd be most useful for those on sentry duty. It's good to hear our magicians are producing things day-to-day useful at last.

TERZKY: But they also dealt in first and last causes, and asked questions like why did God in adorning the Universe heed the difference between the straight and the curved and preferred the nobleness of the curve. They held discussions on the Hermetic texts under the occult rays of the Archangel Michael and they looked at the Tarot card known as the Fool, which is God as the Cosmic Joker and recognized its truth. They saw the richer patterns, invoked the celestial universe under a waning moon and a hundred green candles. In all, they strove to unlock the secrets of the other higher world out there, so as to change this one down here.

HERZBRUDER: This world's not for changing. It's for slaying and being slain, hunting and being hunted, robbing and being robbed, hurting and being hurt – always and for ever.

JACOB: Bbbuuu exxxaaa hoooo iiii haaa thooo eeee gooo thuuuzzz waaa.

HERZBRUDER: Jacob wants to know if the magis found out how we came to these long years of war?

TERZKY: You don't need mighty magi brains for that. Greed's the answer. Limitless greed. The war began when Frederick the Elector of Palatine claimed the throne and territories of Bohemia.

HERZBRUDER: Didn't he have enough?

TERZKY: Whoever has enough?

HERZBRUDER: In the beginning wasn't it still a Church war?

TERZKY: Yes, Catholic versus Protestant. But that soon broke when the French, Walloon, Italian, Spanish, Swedish, Danish, Croat and Irish mercenaries poured in for loot. Now, Catholic France fights Catholic Spain with Papal blessing, and Lutheran Swedes slaughter Lutheran Danes. There's no allegiance left for a religious man to cling to.

HERZBRUDER: When I sign on with an army quartermaster, I want to know how much he pays not how much he prays: Papists, Protestants, Calvinists, Lutherans, Knipperdolling Anabaptists, we've seen too much religion – 'O mine only comfort, my hope, my riches, my God. O simplicity, O ignorance, O gibberish.' My money's on money. It's a god men can rely on for protection. Christ has fled, lucre is in His place.

TERZKY: In the year of Our Lord 1618, when it all began, they killed only for Christ, now they kill for any reason. In that long lost world before the flood it was different. Simonides invented an art perfected by Metrodorus of Skepsis, whereby men and women, by repeating a single word could remember all they had ever seen or heard or read . . . 'Before', 'before', 'before', 'before' is the word that sends me back. I can remember the music and the silk dresses and taffeta ribbons my mother wore and the morning smell of bacon broth and ginger and my father, noble-headed in lace collar, in his library, the finest in all Spessart. My old nurse used to give me quince and lemon drinks in front of the fire of an evening. It was a 'was' and 'every-would-be' world, everything so set, so sure in the bosom of a family; those born after don't know what that means. Then, war came, in the shape of a Swedish foraging party. They sacked the estate, raped and butchered the servants and held my parents prisoners for ransom. I heard later my mother died of jail-fever and my father lost his wits; he believed himself to be the High Admiral of the Bohemian Navy. I war-wandered for years, becoming arse spittle to various major and minor rulers, dependent for my bread on the April weather of a prince's sharky smile. But I remember days before, never again so fine, never again so sure.

HERZBRUDER: We had no silks or taffety. We were peasants, though my father was a householder. He thought we'd escape. No one escapes. The Croats came one summer evening at dusk, looking for gold. They burnt the village to the ground and raped and tortured men, women and children. Years later I caught the Croat commander of that troop, cut off his ears and nose and buried him alive. They threw my father into his own baking oven and lit the fire.

My mother died when they put a cord round her head and twisted it tight with a piece of wood till blood gushed out of her mouth and nose. But 'tisn't the screams of the dying I remember but the song of the nightingales. They didn't stop one note of their sweet, uncaring song for carnage's sake. It took me years to be as naturally uncaring as those nightingales. Before I'd learnt the lesson I married a merchant's daughter, Elise. Three boys born of her soft flesh. She was from Magdeburg.

TERZKY: Ah, Magdeburg . . .

JACOB: Maaaagaa . . .

HERZBRUDER: We had our home there, tables, chairs, doors and windows, real linen on the bed. Her cheeks were rosy, not yet so red as the red garters with which the Swabian waggoners at Ulm truss up their breeches but rosy enough for me. Her eyes shone, hair black, gypsy fingers long and slender . . . neck as white as curdled milk. When Tilly's butchers o'erran Magdeburg, they cut off her head – the easier to snatch the gold necklace round that white, white neck. My boys they threw on to pikes. I'm told it took them three hours a-dying there. And the nightingales sang. Hweet-hweet-tucc-tucc-tucc. When I hear them sing now, 'tis like the word Simonides needs to remember. I remember her and them. It took me years of butchering before I could sing as uncaring as nightingales sing. Hweet-hweet-tucc-tucc-tucc.

JACOB: I I I I I neee nooo wooo soooo tttt reeeeaaa . . . ooohhh . . . iiii waaaa . . . hhhh beeeee zzzz nooo.

HERZBRUDER: He says he needs no words or songs to remember how it was and how it is now.

(JACOB *makes a supreme effort to speak.*)

JACOB: Rrreeee aaahh I I I I waaa yoooo yooo smaaa smaaa moo aaa faaarrr mother aaa father . . . deee deaf . . . I I I I heard fffor theeem . . . aaa . . . sspooaaa ssppook . . . spoke . . . ffffor eeee ththth . . . them . . . spoke for them . . . THEN theee hhheee Hessians caa came . . . aaarrgg . . . thaaa aaaa waaa joke haa aaa aaa . . . they dee deaf maa

made meee dumb . . . deaf aaa dumb fffamily . . .
aaawwhh awa ggg . . . ththth niiii . . . nightingales agghh
urrr . . . (*Singing*) 'Aaaww allaagaa eeehhh tthhhrrr, aaaww
allaagaa eeehh ggrrr.'

HERZBRUDER: He says . . .

TERZKY: I understand what he says.

JACOB: Aa.

HERZBRUDER: Fur-coated, leather-booted you may be but you
understand us. That's a wonder too, Master Count. For
that and the other wonders you've told us of, we endorse
your safe conduct.

TERZKY: My thanks for that mercy.

HERZBRUDER: The fact of it is, 'tis easy enough to slit up a
stranger, he's only so much moving meat. But talk to him
but a little and 'tis more difficult to use the knife. We've
talked too much for killing. Time for you to go, Count.
(*They get up.*)

TERZKY: Good. I am already late and shall be missed.

HERZBRUDER: Of course, we'll take your coat and gloves and
lace collar as keepsakes but leave you your boots. It's a fair
walk to Osnabruck.

(TERZKY *takes off his coat and gloves.*)

TERZKY: Take them with my blessing. All I wish for now is to
get to Osnabruck as soon as possible. I've urgent business
there. I'm acting as envoy extraordinary for the Imperial
Ambassador, Graf von Trauttmansdorf. A Peace
Conference is to be held in Osnabruck and Münster.

HERZBRUDER: They had a Peace Conference in Prague back in
'35 and the war went on. For years they've talked of peace
and made war.

TERZKY: This time there's a change in the weather. We've been
warring for close thirty years, near eighty if you count the
fighting 'twix Spain and the United Provinces. The rulers of
the world're calling a halt. They've more to gain from
peace, so they'll opt for that state.

JACOB: (*Laughing*) Nooooo oooo.

TERZKY: Yes. The peace cast has already set out from distant

23

capitals. Trauttmansdorff and Isaac Volmar stand ready for Frederick II, France is sending Henry d'Orléans and Claude de Mesmes, the Swedes will have John Oxenstierna and Adler Salvius, Spain has the Conde de Penaranda and Antonius Brun. They are too big to be allowed to fail.

HERZBRUDER: 'Tisn't possible.

TERZKY: 'Tis. I am to inform all representatives that the Imperial Frederick agrees with Swedish Queen Christina, it must be peace. And those two hold the key.

JACOB: Peeeace?

TERZKY: 'Stead of ravaging armies, chaos and death, there's a chance for homes, families, law, tranquillity and order.

HERZBRUDER: A chance for the return of the old order in new disguises: old taxes, old chains – church chains, state chains. War and chaos give ordinary men like Jacob and me something we never had before, a chance to be free.

TERZKY: A chance to starve and die.

HERZBRUDER: Freeing yourself is easy, being free is hard but worth every thaler of it. Yes, we die, but war has helped take the terror out of death. It's so commonplace. Bang, you're dead and they pull off your boots, roll you into a hole and it's over. Nobody thinks about it.

JACOB: (*Laughing*) Aaa-aaa.

HERZBRUDER: Yes, we laugh at it. In war we can be what we want to be. We can rise. The swineherd Tamburlaine became the terror of the world, Agathocles, the son of a potter, became King of Sicily. And me, the son of a peasant, became Provost of Harlots and Jacob, Temporary Spymaster for Wrangler's army. No one gets honours and titles without the destruction of others. Nobility is only bought with the ruin of thousands. So time of war is the best time for men like us to rise to a noble title. In peace all ranks're settled.

JACOB: Peeece isss cheeee ooo eeeeaazzz.

HERZBRUDER: Right, peace is never cheap or easy. Count, consider what you and the others do – the world is unprepared to meet the terrible demands of peace. We shall be truly ruined.

TERZKY: We're ruined now, look around you, man, at the ruin; it stretches across and beyond. What could be more ruined than this ruin? Look forward or you'll be left behind.

JACOB: Iiiiffff peeeaaa waaa eeee doooaa?

TERZKY: If there's peace, what do you do? Why, man, you live in peace, that's the goal of most men.

HERZBRUDER: Not never. I ask with Jacob, what do we do? We know how to split a man in two, women also; torture a rich merchant for his hidden gold, kill with a light touch and if possible, a smile. These are singular virtues in war, harshly acquired, highly prized and priced. But these bright shining virtues'll be looked on as darkling sins, punishable in peace. We ask you again, what do we do?

TERZKY: Learn a different song.

JACOB: Ttttooo laaataa.

HERZBRUDER: Too late. We've been too well trained. You princes made the rules we live by, now you seek to change 'em 'cause 'tis profitable. Profit for you means stale bread and begging bowls for us.

TERZKY: You've both suffered – parents, wife, children, tongue cut off; years of misery, slow dying, sudden death. And yet you don't want to end the war. I don't understand!

HERZBRUDER: For us peace would be worse. . . Kill him, Jacob!

(JACOB *fires his pistol, hitting* TERZKY.)

TERZKY: Whaaaa . . . ?

JACOB: Whaaa.

HERZBRUDER: Now they won't know a while that the Imperial Frederick and the Swedish Christina want peace. With luck, your death will delay the dreadful coming of peace a little.

TERZKY: For this . . . you will burn . . . in Hell.

(*He falls.*)

HERZBRUDER: Count, we've been there all our lives.

TERZKY: The moon isn't in place . . . Tried to help . . . but lakes don't flow into anything . . . Confess me . . . In the name of . . .

(*He dies. The lights fade.*)

JACOB: Thhhh . . . aaa Father . . . Sssooo . . . aaa . . . Hhhoo
Holy . . . Ghoooo . . . ooo . . .

HERZBRUDER: Help me throw him in the river.

(*They pick up* TERZKY's *body and carry it Up Stage into the
darkness.* HERZBRUDER *is heard whistling, imitating a
nightingale. There is the sound of the body being thrown into the
river.*)

JACOB: (*Singing*) Aaaaaa . . .

HERZBRUDER: (*Singing*) . . . men

(*They move away with* HERZBRUDER *still whistling. There is
the sound of the river flowing past. That too finally fades.*)

THE REAL LONG JOHN SILVER

HENRY BOWER *hobbles into sight Down Stage Centre as Long John Silver complete with peg-leg, crutch and a stuffed parrot on his shoulder. He speaks in an exaggerated 'Robert Newton' accent.*

HENRY: 'Arr, Jim lad, Jim lad, nigh on six weeks and not a sight of land. Becalmed for days, enough to give you the horrors, what with the heat and all.' (*He lets out a parrot squawk.*) *Pieces of eight! Pieces of eight, ha-ha-ha!* 'Drat that bird!' (*Singing*) 'Fifteen men on a dead man's chest. Yo-ho-ho and a bottle of rum. Drink and the devil have done the rest. Yo-ho-ho and a bottle of rum . . .' (*Calling in his normal voice*) Madge, aren't you ready yet?!
  (*Lights up on suburban living room. Door to bedroom Stage Right, door to hall Stage Left.* MADGE *calls back from the bedroom.*)

MADGE'S VOICE: One more minute and you can see my costume!

HENRY: You can see mine too. It's really good. Hurry, we'll be late!

MADGE'S VOICE: Almost ready!

HENRY: (*To himself*) Yes, I've done well. This must be the best Long John Silver costume ever. Perfect fit down to the wooden leg and parrot. But, of course, I've got the perfect body for it. Cometh the man, cometh the hour. (*Parrot squawk*) *Treasure! Treasure! Treasure! Ha-ha-ha.* 'Drat that bird! I've seen decks running with blood and men mad with the lust for gold. Some was afeard of Blind Pew and some afeard of Captain Flint but all was afeard of me, arr, Jim lad!'

MADGE'S VOICE: I'm ready! Close your eyes. It's a surprise!

HENRY: All right but hurry!
  (*The bedroom door opens and* MADGE BOWER *comes out. She too is dressed as Long John Silver with peg-leg, crutch and stuffed parrot.*)

MADGE: 'Arr, Jim lad, nigh on six weeks and not a sight of . . .'
(*She stops.* MADGE *and* HENRY *contemplate each other in horror.*)

HENRY: Are you trying to be funny?

MADGE: What do you mean, am I trying to be funny?

HENRY: That, that, that costume you've got on. That's a Long John Silver costume!

MADGE: And that, that, that. What about that, that, that costume you've got on? That's Long John Silver, too, if I'm not mistaken. You said we won't tell each other what costumes we're going to wear so it'll be a surprise. It's your fault!

HENRY: Oh God, I was in such a good mood this evening. I don't care whose fault it is, we can't both turn up in the same fancy dress costume. You'll have to change.

MADGE: Why me? Why do I have to change?

HENRY: Why? Why? Because you look like an unmade bed: you're ludicrous.

MADGE: Ludicrous?! This costume cost forty-six pounds plus VAT to hire. See. I've got my wooden leg, crutch, cutlass, hat and parrot. It's perfect.

HENRY: Perfect? How can it be perfect? Long John Silver was a salty old sea-dog who cocked his leg up anywhere.

MADGE: That's why I'm going to win first prize. How many years have we been going to the Guildford and Godalming Fancy Dress – five? six? This time I'm winning something. There'll be no Long John Silvers in the women's section – except me.

HENRY: Of course not because Long John Silver was a *man*.

MADGE: Rhoda Chappel won first prize last year as Lord Byron.

HENRY: Rhoda Chappel has a great pair of legs. Those white breeches and black leather boots were very becoming.

MADGE: A man dressed as Long John Silver is ordinary but a woman, that's special.

HENRY: You'll never win anything. You haven't got the shape for it. You're top heavy and your cutlass is hanging round your knees. And it's not just a matter of looking wrong.

You've got to be in character. 'Arr, Jim lad – nigh on six weeks and not a sight of land. I've seen decks running with blood and men mad with the lust for gold, arr.'

MADGE: 'Arr, Jim lad, nigh on six weeks and not a sight of land. I've seen decks running with blood and men mad with the lust for gold, arr.'

HENRY: (*Parrot squawk*) *Pieces of eight*! *Pieces of eight, ha-ha-ha*! 'Drat that bird!'

MADGE: (*Parrot squawk*) *Pieces of eight*! *Pieces of eight, ha-ha-ha*! 'Drat that bird!'

HENRY: (*Singing*) 'Fifteen men on a dead man's chest. Yo-ho-ho and a bottle of rum. Drink and the devil have done the rest. Yo-ho-ho and a bottle of rum.'

MADGE: (*Singing*) 'Fifteen men on a dead man's chest. Yo-ho-ho and a bottle of rum. Drink and the devil have done the rest. Yo-ho-ho and a bottle of rum.'

HENRY: It's terrible.

MADGE: It's marvellous.

HENRY: It's a million and a half miles from the real Long John Silver.

MADGE: You know the real Long John?

HENRY: Yes. Yes. He was a true swashbuckler. He murdered and betrayed. He lived life full to the brim and then some. He was a gorgeous colourful character. You could never be that Long John.

MADGE: And you could? The only colourful thing about you is your varicose veins. As chief cashier for Parsons and Penrose for the last twenty years, you've made our life so dull I actually look forward to dental appointments.

HENRY: So criticize, you've gone through your life pushing doors marked 'pull'.

MADGE: I'm not going to waste my breath on you.

HENRY: I wouldn't, natural gas is expensive.

MADGE: If our relationship was any good, you'd've known I was going as Long John without me having to say a word.

HENRY: Don't you know what Long John means to me? When the costume arrived from Berman's, it was like a revelation.

I saw the sun again. Oh yes, I eat my cheese and Marmite sandwiches every day and catch the six forty-three home every evening. And these four walls go on being four. My life's a form of petrified dreaming, I'm stiff with the cares and worries of it. But deep down, Long John Silver is the true me – mean, murderous and magnificent. 'Arr, Jim lad, we live rough and risk swinging at noon . . .' I'm not giving him up; not ever, 'Arr, arr, arr.'

MADGE: I'm certainly not going to. I've made enough sacrifices. My life's housework and housework in that order. I've dwindled down to a Mrs. I know now there are two kinds of people in the world – me and all the others. You're not getting Long John Silver.

HENRY: I've got him. I'm Long John. Nobody stands in my way. 'Arr, Jim lad, some was afeard of Blind Pew and some was afeard of Captain Flint but all was afeard of me.'

MADGE: (*Parrot squawk*) *Afeard of you?! Afeard of you, ha-ha-ha*! You fainted three times at our wedding.

HENRY: It didn't help, I still had to marry you.

MADGE: You say that but what would you do without me?!

HENRY: Better! I feel a torrent in me now that can't be bottled. Long John Silver's the key. I'm fifty and I'm as good as I was at twenty.

MADGE: God – that gives me some idea how good you were at twenty.

HENRY: Don't underestimate me, Madge.

MADGE: That's not possible. . . . I'm a winner, Henry.
(HENRY *stumps away and crashes into a chair*.)
Careful where you put your peg-leg!

HENRY: 'Arr, Jim lad, she don't have to worry none about my peg-leg, do she? We're going as Long John Silver, ain't we, Jim lad? Arr, we are.'

MADGE: You're not, I am, aren't I? (*Parrot squawk*) *Yes, she's going as Long John Silver, she's going, ha-ha-ha*!

HENRY: You're not, 'arr!'

MADGE: I am, 'arr'! Right then, we'll let George decide.

HENRY: George? Why George?

MADGE: Because he's coming round to pick us up any minute. He can choose who's the best Long John.

HENRY: Oh, you'd like that, wouldn't you? . . . 'Arr, Jim lad, she'd like that' . . . You'd just flutter what's left of your eyelashes and he'll pick you . . . 'Arr, Jim lad, we can see, we're not blind like Blind Pew . . .' We know.

MADGE: We know what?

HENRY: We know what we know about you and George.

MADGE: (*Parrot squawk*) *Stupid! Stupid! Ha-ha-ha! He's so stupid* . . . I keep telling you there's nothing between George and me. I haven't liked him much ever since he started parting his hair in the middle. But he's been a friend since before we were married.

HENRY: I know all about your Tuesday afternoon trips into Guildford: cups of Kenco at the Kardomah, tête-à-tête. Don't deny it! (*Parrot squawk*) *He knows, he knows ha-ha-ha*!

MADGE: You're mad, sick or worse. It's all those cheese and Marmite sandwiches. How can you even think it? George Basildon is Deputy Area Supervisor Grade II for South Eastern Gas!

HENRY: I smile, I smile, I smile.

MADGE: You can smile till your teeth crack. It won't change anything, will it, Poll? (*Parrot squawk*) *It won't change anything ha-ha-ha*!

HENRY: 'I knows what I know, arr, Jim lad.' I'm not saying anything much happens in Guildford necessarily. Nothing much ever happens in Guildford. But don't tell me George isn't biased; he's been got at over the years, pressures, pressures.

MADGE: All right, we won't ask George who's the best Long John Silver.

HENRY: So you can turn round and say I didn't want George to choose because I was frightened he wouldn't choose me. Of course, if he doesn't choose me, we'll all know the reason why, won't we? Nobody in their right mind would pick you as the better man.

MADGE: If you're the better man, I'm a Lebanese juggler.

HENRY: I fill the space. I'm the one and only Long John Silver.

MADGE: There's only one one-and-only Long John Silver in this house!

HENRY: And that's me!

(*There is a knock on the door.*)

MADGE: And that's George.

HENRY: Right, we'll give him a chance then . . . (*Calling*) It's open, George! The latch is off! . . . We'll see his first instinctive reaction. That'll tell us a lot.

MADGE: Just let me get my parrot straight.

(*They hop into position.*)

HENRY: No prompting.

(*The front door is heard being closed. Pause. Then there is the tell-tale sound of a peg-leg tapping menacingly on the ground as* GEORGE *stumps slowly forward towards the living room.*)

MADGE: It can't be . . .

HENRY: It's an epidemic.

(*The living room door is flung open and* GEORGE BASILDON *bursts in as Long John Silver.*)

GEORGE: 'Arr, Jim lad, nigh on six weeks and not a sight of . . .' (*He stops in horror at the sight of the other two Long Johns.*) Are you trying to be funny?

HENRY: Funny?

GEORGE: I'm Long John Silver this year. See, I've got my wooden leg, crutch, cutlass, hat and parrot. Why the devil didn't you tell me?

HENRY: Why didn't you?

GEORGE: There's no point in talking, I'm going as Long John Silver. I've made up my mind. We'll be laughed at if you go as well. You'll have to change.

HENRY: *I'll* have to change.

GEORGE: Of course, I look more like Long John than you do.

HENRY: How can you look more like Long John than I do?

GEORGE: Because my parrot's bigger than yours . . . (*Parrot squawk*) *Pieces of eight! Pieces of eight, ha-ha-ha!* 'Drat that bird!'

HENRY: Yours is sick. Psittacosis – parrot fever! Parrot fever!

GEORGE: It's a trick of the light. 'Drat that bird.'

HENRY: It's dead and it's moulting all over the carpet. (*Parrot squawk*) *Ha-ha-ha.*

(MADGE, *who has been hopping up and down with impatience, finally barges in between them.*)

MADGE: George, George, what about me, George?!

GEORGE: You look like an uncooked army boot.

HENRY: Don't talk to my wife like that . . . I thought she looked like an unmade bed. But you're right, she does look more like an uncooked army boot.

GEORGE: I'm sorry, Madge, I'm a bit unnerved. The sight of you two wobbling around on wooden legs . . . Now Madge, I've been a friend for fifteen years and I've got to tell you the truth. Madge, you're a woman.

HENRY: I've told her that but she won't listen, she's obsessed. She's having trouble knowing what she is – animal or mineral. She's lost touch with reality.

MADGE: I know who's lost touch. George – Henry thinks you're my lover.

GEORGE: Really, Madge, Henry knows I'm Deputy Area Supervisor Grade II for South Eastern Gas!

HENRY: Of course. It's the first thing I pointed out to her. It's all part of it . . .

MADGE: What?!

GEORGE: Madge, it's no good getting emotional; it's not our way. This is a crisis and it must be approached logically. It's obvious it would be better if only one of us went as Long John Silver. Now, there's no time for elaborate costume changes so I suggest you two go as something simple, like a tramp or nudist.

MADGE: Nudist? What would people say if I turned up in the Crystal Room of the Guildford Arms stark naked?

HENRY: They'd say I'd married you for your money. You and George can go as something else, but I've got my character.

MADGE: I had the idea first, so I'm not saying please or thank you. I owe it to myself . . . Anyway George, how can you

35

be Long John Silver with glasses? And they're horn-rimmed! (*Parrot squawk*) *Four eyes! Four eyes, ha-ha-ha!* 'Drat that bird!'

GEORGE: Horn-rimmed or tortoise-shelled, glasses don't make any difference. I don't really need them except that I can't see without 'em. Glasses aren't here or there. It's not only a matter of how you look, it's always being in character that's important.

MADGE: 'Arr, Jim lad, he's raving. I've seen men go mad with the lust for gold.'

GEORGE: A gas main bursts, a gas cooker's faulty, a radiator springs a leak, I rush a team from South Eastern Gas to the spot . . . Those men go without a second thought. They don't look back; eyes straight ahead, jaws firm. They risk death and mutilation daily – on my orders. Why? Why? Because . . . 'some was afeard of Blind Pew and some was afeard of Captain Flint but all was afeard of me.'

HENRY: (*Parrot squawk*) *Willie Wet Leg, Willie Wet Leg, ha-ha-ha!* They used to call you Willie Wet Leg at school and you never changed.

GEORGE: (*Parrot squawk*) *Shiver my timbers! Shiver my timbers, ha-ha-ha!* You've asked for it!
(*He hops over to* HENRY *and knocks the parrot off his shoulder.*)

HENRY: (*Parrot squawk*) *Arrrkk. Arrrkk* . . . You see that, Madge, he's knocked my parrot off.

MADGE: Knock his off then. (*Parrot squawk*) *Ha-ha-ha!*
(HENRY *stumps over and knocks* GEORGE's *parrot off his shoulder.*)

GEORGE: (*Parrot squawk*) *Arrrhh. Arrrhh.* He's knocked my parrot off!

MADGE: (*Parrot squawk*) *Ha-ha-ha!* That's better.

GEORGE: What do we do now?

HENRY: Knock hers off!
(*They quickly stump over to* MADGE *and knock her parrot off her shoulder on to the floor.*)

MADGE: (*Parrot squawk*) *Send for Blind Pew. Blind Pew. Aarrkk, aarrkk!*

ALL: 'Drat that bird!'

GEORGE: I've had enough of paying excess fare at the end of the journey like an honest man. I sit at my desk at South Eastern Gas and think of the Mongols with their wild horses and their towers of skulls. (*He suddenly starts laughing.*)

HENRY: 'You can laugh, by thunder, but those that die'll be the lucky ones, arr, Jim lad.'

GEORGE: I'm laughing because it's no contest. You're born losers. Only this Long John Silver will be showing himself tonight.

HENRY: Why?

GEORGE: It's my car and there's only room for one!

HENRY: After all we've done for you! Just look around – high speed gas-cooker, gas fridge, full gas central heating. The whole place is a monument to gas. Damn your eyes, Basildon, we're changing to electric.

MADGE: So you're taking the golden road to Guildford and leaving us behind? All the years of friendship blasted and betrayed.

GEORGE: Yes, yes, yes, because – I'm the real Long John Silver and betraying is my business. A leopard never changes his spots!

HENRY: (*Pulling out his pistol*) Right! You see this pistol, I'm pointing it straight at you. Unscrew your leg or I'll drop you where you stand.

MADGE: (*Parrot squawk*) *Cut him to pieces, ha-ha-ha!*

GEORGE: 'Arr, Jim lad, they can't stop Long John Silver with threats, not never.'

HENRY: The price of freedom is blood! You asked for this bullet; it has your name on it, George Basildon . . . (*He pulls the trigger. There is a loud click and nothing happens.*) Damn British workmanship!

MADGE: It's like you, defective.

GEORGE: We villains bear charmed lives. The devil protects his own.

HENRY: I never give up. See . . .

(GEORGE *laughs as* HENRY *pulls the trigger again. This time*

37

the pistol fires. MADGE *screams.* GEORGE *stops laughing and gasps.*)

GEORGE: Henry . . . Madge . . .

MADGE: (*Sobbing*) George!

GEORGE: (*Gasping*) 'Arr . . . arr . . . arr . . . Jim lad, this time they've done for me . . . the old sea-dog takes his last bow . . .' (*He staggers to* HENRY.) Shoot me again, Henry, I love the smell of gunpowder and cordite. (*He stamps his peg-leg.*) 'Some was afeard of Blind Pew and some was afeard of Captain Flint but all was afeard of me.' Time for me to go.

(*Cries of rage from* HENRY *and* MADGE.)

MADGE: Stop him!

HENRY: The car keys!

(*They dive at him. There is a crash as they all fall.*)

MADGE: I must win!

GEORGE: No pity!

HENRY: Stop breathing my air!

(*The three roll on the floor fighting.*)

GEORGE: Henry! Madge! Look at the time.

(*They stop fighting.*)

MADGE: What?

GEORGE: No point now. It's started . . . we're too late . . .

HENRY: Ohhhh . . .

MADGE: All gone down . . .

(*They get up slowly.*)

GEORGE: I wanted . . . I wanted to be a great villain for a night . . . but this country's always lacked tyrants, never slaves . . . I wanted to fill my declining weekends with a dream of glory . . . 'Arr, Jim, Jim.'

MADGE: I wanted . . . I wanted to throw off for a night, this skin that doesn't fit me . . . but if you're wedlocked and weak it destroys your mentals . . . I wanted to win instead of living a borrowed life knitting mittens . . . 'Arr, Jim, Jim.'

HENRY: I wanted . . . I wanted to stand up straight for a night instead of clasping my hands together, panting in a cage . . . I wanted to leave my mark on this world . . . we give ourselves a role to play so as to have some pretext for living and mine was taken from me . . . 'Arr, Jim Jim.' (*They gently sing and dance, tapping out the tune with their peg-legs.*)

HENRY
MADGE } : (*Singing*)
GEORGE

    'We struck out for the sea, sea, sea.
    But it was not to be, be, be.
    We wanted to be bold, bold, bold,
    To start breaking the mould, mould, mould.
    But life is so grey, grey, grey.
    Dribbles away, away, away.
    Now we're lost and we're cold,
    And we'll all soon be old . . .'
    'Arr, Jim lad.'

THE HEIRS OF DIOGENES

A yard outside the temple of Cybele. Corinth, 335 BC. DIOGENES
crouches in a large barrel. CRATES *stands beside him.*

CRATES: I'm your devoted disciple, Diogenes, but arriving back
at Corinth I'm shocked to find you, one of the greatest
philosophers of his time, living in this luxury.

DIOGENES: This luxury, spindle-shanks! Luxury? I'm living as
I've always lived, bareheaded, barefooted, in rags and in a
barrel. A *barrel*. It's been my home for the last fifteen years.
For fifteen years I've been in a barrel!

CRATES: Man isn't a snail or hermit-crab. He doesn't need
barrels. Barrels are superfluous.

DIOGENES: I live in a barrel and I smashed my last water-bowl
when I saw a boy drinking from the hollow of his hand. I
have nothing.

CRATES: I *am* nothing.

DIOGENES: I eat roots, scraps, lie under torn sacking.

CRATES: In Athens, I lie naked in excrement, suck dry fish-
bones and rotten olives.

DIOGENES: This is Corinth, most here are too poor to afford fish
and too thrifty to let olives rot. Just as I tried to outdo my
teacher, Arististhes, so you to me in your turn: so sons
consume their fathers. But never say I have forsaken the
tenets of the true philosophy which is the hope of the
world. I still believe, virtue is knowledge and virtue consists
in rejecting all physical pleasure. Hardship is necessary in
achieving goodness and we must return to nature and
simplicity.

CRATES: What you believe and what you practise, diverge,
Diogenes. A man should be able to hold out his hand to a
friend without closing his fingers into a fist. But I cannot. I see
you've gone soft at the edges. You betray your own doctrine.

DIOGENES: Betray it? I live it, sparrow-mouth! Even Plato
never suggests that and he hates me because I once asked

43

him for a few figs and he sent me a whole jar. I told him 'If
I asked you what two and two are, you don't answer
twenty.' Nowadays, Plato only hears the sound of applause.

CRATES: I hear you suffer from the same affliction.

DIOGENES: Wrong from the start! When they come to flatter me
with fat livings in the academies of Thebes, Athens and
Sparta, I drive them off, barking like a dog, *grrrr*! *Grrrr*!

CRATES: You bark like a dog, I live like one. At first I taught
like you. I was called 'Door-Opener' because I went into
every house and gave advice. But then I asked what did I
gain from teaching philosophy? Nothing but a peck of lupin
seeds I carry with me to make me fart. So now I wander the
streets bare-arsed naked, clothed only in my dirt. I rub my
body against the walls to clean myself as asses do. My
eyes're rheumy with Attic dust, my skin is covered with
swellings. I scratch myself with nails never trimmed and
from this affliction I draw a double profit since I wear them
down with my scratching to relieve my itch.

DIOGENES: I heard such rumours of you but didn't believe
them. In your zeal to out-zeal your old teacher you fall into
error: pride and pleasure come in many forms, masked as
pain and misery.

CRATES: There's no pride or pleasure for me in scrambling in
the offal pits of the city with starving dogs. Despite their
terrible hunger they never harmed me. We remain stray
dogs together.

DIOGENES: Good. I like it. You haven't forgotten my teaching
that one strong picture is worth a thousand words, words,
words of philosophy. Now, man and starving dogs living in
harmony is a picture that leaches the imagination. People
are indifferent to good words but if I whistle and dance like
a demented goat, men gather. It's why I live in a barrel;
why I go to the market at noon with a lighted lantern,
looking for an honest man; why I beg stone statues for food
to get used to always being refused like the poor. Diogenes
and his barrel, Diogenes and his lantern, Diogenes and his
statues. These teaching pictures men and women will

remember after my words are long gone, dead in the air.

CRATES: I have no need of teaching pictures and such stupidities. I no longer teach. Your desire to reform men's morals is another form of pride.

DIOGENES: You dare criticize me, you gap-toothed nidget! You are on trial here. You bring my Cynic's doctrine into disrepute. Even in this provincial barrel, I hear all the dirt about you. Is it true you consort in the streets of Athens with a woman called Hipparchia?

CRATES: No. I never consort. I married her. Hipparchia is my wife.

DIOGENES: It's true then! You are dedicated to denying all physical pleasure and this action is all pleasure!

CRATES: You're not married, Diogenes, or you wouldn't say that. Marriage is one more hardship.

DIOGENES: Socrates was of that mind too. Why did you take her to wife?

CRATES: Nothing would turn her away, not my ugliness, poverty or horror of my outward life. When she threatened to kill herself, her family relented and so did I.

DIOGENES: There's another accusation current – when the fancy takes you, you take her publicly in the streets as dogs do bitches.

CRATES: I warned her that nothing in our lives together would be hidden.

DIOGENES: That's true then?!

CRATES: After we'd wed we were followed for weeks by crowds expecting us to conduct our nuptials in public. Nothing draws a crowd faster or keeps it longer than the prospect of sexual practices. They were disappointed, the fancy rarely took me and never in public.

DIOGENES: Does this wife go naked, too?

CRATES: I believe so, but she has very long hair.

DIOGENES: Crates, Crates, I trained you for the study of the great questions of life and death.

CRATES: I studied them and found them wanting. I only study my body now. And that which is necessary to it. I strive to

cut off those necessities one by one. The great questions
don't concern me as I crawl to oblivion.

DIOGENES: Man is not a snail or hermit-crab, neither is he a
worm. What mad pride possesses you to cavort in the
streets, dirt-naked with a hairy wife and starving dogs?
You're lost, Crates, lost.

CRATES: You are lost, Diogenes. I knew before I came: old and
cowering low in a barrel, rotten with compromise. I'm the
one to take up the torch, carry the banner whether you
deny me or not, I am your heir.

(*A fanfare of trumpets.*)

DIOGENES: What have we now? Some young fool coming to see
me. It's become fashionable to complete your education by
visiting Diogenes in his barrel. Look at his white plume and
armour shining like the rays of heat at noonday.

CRATES: He gleams, riding on the wave-crest of youth, strong,
fresh and *clean*. See how clean he is. It's this Greek
obsession with indiscriminate bathing that is the cause of
our woes.

(ALEXANDER *enters Stage Left.*)

ALEXANDER: Greetings, Diogenes.

DIOGENES: I'm already bored. Quicker, man.

ALEXANDER: No, this moment should be savoured. Two of the
greatest men of their time meet at last.

DIOGENES: Two? Who's the other? Who are you?

ALEXANDER: The son of King Philip of Macedonia and Queen
Olympia . . . Alexander. I am Alexander the Great.

DIOGENES: Ye gods, what some men will say to scrape up an
acquaintance. Alexander, or whatever you choose to call
yourself, a man may appear a fool and yet not be one. He
may just be guarding his wisdom carefully. But that doesn't
apply in your case. You do not impress me by calling
yourself Alexander. Go thy ways.

CRATES: Pull down thy vanity, young man, pull down.

ALEXANDER: Who're you?

CRATES: Crates. I eat lupin seeds.

ALEXANDER: I eat the whole world and still I'm hungry. I can't

46

see the frontiers of my soul. If I were fire, I'd burn the earth, if I were water, I'd drown it. I desire to be so great that man coming after will never believe that I existed, so beautiful, so powerful, that they will only be able to think of me as an idea. Like the gods, I think of myself as inconceivable.

CRATES: Soft, soft, I hear in that, shattered stones, falling masonry, the ruin of space, time and the world.

DIOGENES: Then, you are then, truly Alexander the Great . . . Disappointing. A man pretending to be Alexander the Great shows imagination and a man with imagination is redeemable. But you don't pretend to be, you are what you say you are, Alexander. There's no imagination there, just dull facts. What do you want from me?

ALEXANDER: It's what you want from me. I've been a devoted disciple of yours ever since the day I heard the story of how you were captured by pirates and sold as a slave in Crete. In the slave market you were asked your trade and you said, 'Governing men. Sell me to a man who needs a master.' Masterly.

DIOGENES: I'm deafened by the clanking chains of my youthful pride. I regret that reply.

ALEXANDER: It's a reply worthy of an Alexander. As master of the Aegean, I ask is there anything you want from me?

DIOGENES: Yes, one thing – step out of my sunlight. You're standing between me and the sun.

ALEXANDER: 'You're standing between me and the sun.' You want your share of sunlight. It's an answer to be inscribed in the chronicles of my reign. If I wasn't Alexander, I'd want to be Diogenes.

DIOGENES: That's something else for the chronicles. 'Twill serve you well, help make you out to be the thinking man's tyrant.

ALEXANDER: But I am. Aristotle told me I could've been a teacher of men if I hadn't decided to be a butcher of 'em. Aristotle was a teacher but not an inspirer. You were – are – Diogenes. I've followed your doctrine since I was young.

47

DIOGENES: Why?

ALEXANDER: My father was wild, sensual, everybody's friend
and favourite king. I couldn't be like that. I could only
outdo him by being opposite. So I built my life on your
precepts, Diogenes, control, prohibitions, contempt for the
body and its pleasures. Men like depriving themselves
almost as much as pleasuring themselves: there are as many
misers as gluttons at life's banquet. The pleasures of bed
and board are unworthy – no worse – dangerous handicaps.
Like you, Diogenes, I cast away everything that would
hamper me in my purpose, greed, hate, love, pity, every
compromising fondness.

DIOGENES: What purpose? To become virtuous?

ALEXANDER: No, to become a steel blade to cut the arteries of
this world so it bleeds. I'll rule from the Upper Nile to the
Indus, from Samarkand to Babylon and beyond; from the
Caspian to the Red Sea. Egypt, Assyria and Babylon will be
mine. The Lydians, Phrygians, Armenians, Jews,
Hyrcanians, Parthians, Bactrians and their capitals, wealth
and gods will be subject to my will. I'll be a god myself.

DIOGENES: We have enough gods already. And I curse them all
for making us miserable by raising our eyes to the empty
heavens. Since the gods've decided we must eat, they
should've turned our eyes back to the earth where roots
grow: we can't feed on air, eat the stars.

ALEXANDER: I'll turn them back. I'll simplify men's lives. I can
do what you cannot. No compromise is admirable in
abstract, Diogenes, but it doesn't win enough converts. Just
as honesty is the best policy only when you've no choice.
You've stayed too uncompromisingly hard to reach a wider
audience. So crouch in your barrel, old friend, whilst I
carry your message across the torn world.

DIOGENES: Why?

ALEXANDER: You teach that a man exists for himself alone, he
has no country, knows no man-made frontiers. I, too, want
to make all nations one, under me . . . Besides, you'll give
my conquests an intellectual respectability that could prove

useful. In return, I'll make yours the world philosophy. I'll be your champion and true heir.

DIOGENES: This great universalist, Crates, here, has already declared himself my heir, whatever I say. I wanted to bring mankind the salvation of virtue. You two bring it the salvation of blood and dirt. You in your soul-soaring pride and splendour, you in your flesh crawling humility and squalor. So the most competes with the least.

ALEXANDER: I don't compete. If I want it, it is: the cause is my will alone. I'll be your heir, give you prestige and influence beyond your darkest barrel dreams.

CRATES: And your teachings will be dead before you, Diogenes. Right thinking can't be enforced, philosophy suffocates in power. He offers massacres. Charon's single barge will be too small to ferry his dead to the Stygian shore, fleets will be needed. I'll not compete with this blood-beaked deformity who opens the gates of Hell.

ALEXANDER: You puny sack of excrement.

(*He draws his sword loudly.*)

CRATES: Hear it? It's the sound of Hell's gates opening.

ALEXANDER: No, it's the sound of my sword, unsheathed. Nothing stands against the cutting sword.

CRATES: Useless against the cutting mind.

ALEXANDER: Aristotle and the rest wouldn't agree: they trembled before it.

CRATES: Because they had something to lose. I've nothing.

ALEXANDER: Except your life. How long is it good for a man to live?

CRATES: Just as long as he doesn't prefer death to life.

ALEXANDER: And I'm certain you prefer life, such as it is. Then my sword is still effective.

CRATES: Stay back. The defenceless have their defences, deep within me. You've been warned, Alexander. I breathe straight into your face . . . paaaa!

(*He breathes into* ALEXANDER's *face, who staggers back, gasping.*)

ALEXANDER: Uggh, the stench. I can't breathe.

CRATES: And I have a stronger weapon from my other cavity –
the wind that stinks.

ALEXANDER: No! Keep it sheathed!

CRATES: You still have things to learn, Alexander: no man is
defenceless, if he puts his mind to it.

ALEXANDER: A good lesson, well taught: expect the
unexpected.

CRATES: Sheathe your sword. You kill thousands in forgotten
battles, the bones of your dead bleached in piles. That's
why you're called 'great'. But to kill one naked man,
cold . . .

ALEXANDER: Then I'll be pricked down as a murderous
madman. I destroyed Thebes, men, women and children all
down, down, down. Understood – a stern necessity, setting
an example to deter others. But killing you would be
personal, no higher purpose. Worse, it would be a pleasure.
Against my principles to enjoy it. (*He sheathes his sword.*) So
I'll sheathe my sword but I'll still smash you flat.

CRATES: I am already flatter than you could ever smash. Vain
man, having nothing I am invulnerable.

ALEXANDER: Crow bait, having everything I am invincible.

CRATES: Alexander, now hear the terrible truth. You're less
than the ghost of a louse. For me, you don't exist.

ALEXANDER: I exist for me in myself alone. So I am Diogenes's
only true heir.

CRATES: I am that, for I am a true athlete of righteousness.

DIOGENES: I've spawned monsters. Everyone is a fingertip from
madness: there's a crack in the universe. When I died I
wanted to be buried face down because I thought soon
everything would be turned upside down and righteousness
would prevail. I thought those who came after would be
better. Wrong! What can the comforting deception of
philosophy signify in the face of truth, which is always the
same – nothing ends well. I should've studied emptiness,
nothing, instead of virtue. The gods tried to tell me. One
night I was huddled in my barrel, trying to sleep. The snow
was falling outside and I heard the gods praising me for my

discussion on emptiness, nothing. 'But I haven't said anything,' I told them. 'You haven't said anything as we haven't heard anything: that's true emptiness,' they replied. I should've studied emptiness and midwives should give up their calling; it's a crime against mankind to inflict life on another human being. I look on you two and despair eats the soul. I'd throw away my books but I haven't got any; break my staff but I've never had one; renounce my world but I already have. It's hard to make a gesture that's meaningful when your life's suddenly without meaning. All I can do is go back deeper into my barrel, into the darkness. (*As he edges back down into the barrel, his voice echoes hollowly.*) Back into the darkness . . . no men here . . . all darkness . . . don't follow me . . . alone in darkness, alone . . . crouch down in darkness . . . curl brown at the edges . . . become dry autumn leaf . . . dryer . . . dryer, crumbling into dust . . . dooown . . . dooown . . .

CRATES: Diogenes, what're you doing?

(ALEXANDER *bangs on the sides of the barrel.*)

ALEXANDER: Diogenes, we still have to talk.

DIOGENES: (*Voice echoing*) Talk, then . . .

ALEXANDER: I'm not scraping the bottom of the barrel to talk to you.

CRATES: It means we'll have to stick our heads in the barrel. Even grovelling dirt-naked in the offal pits of Athens, I still had my dignity. I grovelled there because I wanted to. But I don't want to share a barrel with you.

ALEXANDER: I certainly don't. (*Banging the barrel*) Come out!

DIOGENES: (*Voice echoing*) If you don't want to talk, put the lid on and go your ways.

ALEXANDER: Put the lid on – it's tempting. Come, we'll make one more effort to conduct a rational discussion. Crates, I'll put my head in if you will.

CRATES: So be it. Dignity, too, is unnecessary. Heads in!

(*They put their heads and shoulders into the barrel to talk to* DIOGENES.)

ALEXANDER: (*Voice echoing*) This is the gratitude I get for offering you the world. But it will always be so, I offer too much.

CRATES: (*Voice echoing*) I offer too little, it seems. You can't face the natural outcrop of your teaching about body and self-interest, Diogenes. This is how it ends, in pure animalism and will.

DIOGENES: (*Voice echoing*) You are my mistakes. I spit on my mistakes.

ALEXANDER: (*Voice echoing*) He spat in my face!

CRATES: (*Voice echoing*) And mine.

DIOGENES: (*Voice echoing*) I couldn't find a worse place to spit than in your faces. I make no distinction. I study philosophy so I can end up looking at world conquerors and naked nidgets in the same light.

(ALEXANDER *takes his head out of the barrel*.)

ALEXANDER: I don't. I'm not the same as him.

(CRATES *takes his head out of the barrel*.)

CRATES: And I'm not the same as Alexander. I'm better.

(DIOGENES *pops his head out of the barrel*.)

DIOGENES: Gap-toothed nockys, I'm closing up shop. If my philosophy ends in you two being my natural intellectual heirs, I want none of it. Such pride overwhelms the universe. There must be something wrong. I said self-knowledge is the key to virtue, goodness. I know a horse from a mule, a hawk from a hacksaw, a birch from a willow. I know the sayings of Socrates. I know the sun isn't hollow and Atlantis is a dream. I know all manner of things except myself. And even if I knew, knowledge is no guarantee of justice, much less virtue. The only way to keep out of mischief is crouching all day in a barrel.

ALEXANDER: I need no one. All roads lead back to me. As long as I live, the world's mine and under my foot. I need no one.

CRATES: I don't either. My humility makes me invulnerable. Naked and unashamed. I abase myself and defy the heavens.

(*It begins to rain.*)

DIOGENES: They weep. Drive them off, you gods. I want peace.
(*It rains harder.*)

ALEXANDER: There's nothing here for me, except a weak old
man. Not worth my white plume getting wet.

CRATES: We agree on that. There's nothing here now. The
rain's washing away my hard-won dirt. I'm cold.
(*They move off.*)

ALEXANDER: Come away! Why is it that everyone I meet turns
out to be such a disappointment except me?
(*They hurry off. The rain continues.* DIOGENES *pulls the barrel
lid towards him.*)

DIOGENES: Merkin stinkards! Groin lousy churls! (*He pulls the
lid to block the entrance of the barrel.*) Put the lid on . . . tight
. . . die in the dark, dreaming of virtue and goodness . . .
So . . . so . . . Goodnight!
(*The lid is dragged into place with a bang, sealing the barrel
tight. The rain falls remorselessly.*)

SISTERS

IRENE CROSBY *lies in a hospital bed. Her two sisters,* BARBARA *and* KATHERINE *are at her bedside.*

IRENE: Dying alone would be boring. That's why I've asked you two to keep me company. After all, you are my only sisters.

BARBARA: You're not dying, Irene.

KATHERINE: Not now, not yet, not ever.

IRENE: True. I'll only die when I want to. Grumbling is defecation of the soul. I must stop but when the nurses here look at me, I feel I'm just taking up space and they need the bed. Wrap her in a sheet and trundle her to the mortuary. Still, they have a tough job cleaning out the dog kennels every day. So many women fall for the serving suffering humanity routine – fine – but why should suffering humanity have to be served on the cheap? In better times I'd've help organize them but most days now I'm underwater. I'm seventy-five and just look at these for a pair of arms. I tossed a sparrow for them and lost. I'm lucky the needle's in fashion in this hospital. A jab a day keeps the pain away – but not today, girls. My joints'll soon be on fire but I want to be beaver-bright for you. So I'm abstaining in your honour. How goes the world, Barbara?

BARBARA: I think it goes a lot easier now you're laid low.
(*They laugh.*)

KATHERINE: But, Irene, this really is a chance for you to take a rest. You've been working all your life.

IRENE: Most people have to – ever since He threw that pair out of Eden. No matter how it dulls the senses, breaks the spirit, you work or starve: no one smiles on Monday.

BARBARA: You could've done. With your brains you could've been an academic and not worked at all.

IRENE: Can you really see me dreaming my life away amongst dreamy spires? Think of what I'd've missed. I've always

57

been a full-time socialist but I've also been a part-time cook, saleswoman, factory worker, packer, truck driver, spot welder and waitress.

KATHERINE: You as a waitress was a sight to see. That was the time George and I turned up at the Coq d'Or and found you serving at our table. And I said, 'Why are you working as a waitress?'

IRENE: And I said, 'Why – don't you think you're good enough to be served by me?'

KATHERINE: George thought it was funny and you told him the food was under-cooked and over-priced. Then it got political and you were fired. What a trouble you've been to us, Irene. But I was stupid to have been embarrassed. I was young then and didn't understand George saying we had too much money and had it too long ever to be embarrassed.

IRENE: George had style as well as money. You were lucky there, Kathy. Just as you were lucky I spent so much time abroad, otherwise there would've been a few other embarrassing meetings.

KATHERINE: It would've been worth it. As a family we spent so many of the good years on different sides of the world. I understand itchy feet. I always wanted to go to India. Everybody has so many intense spiritual experiences there. The air is so dry.

IRENE: Malnutrition, dirt and disease. Nothing spiritual about it. I've been there.

BARBARA: Fifty years wandering. Why didn't you spend more time in England, Irene?

IRENE: I found the air difficult to breathe. Ever since the Norman Conquest the English have had the habit of obedience. Servility is a national trait, forelock touching a national pastime, everything is done from a kneeling position. So I went to find places where people weren't afraid to fight back . . . And I tried to help.

KATHERINE: Did you?

IRENE: Who knows? I did see a couple of successful

revolutions. Even if those, too, went wrong in the end. No, despite all the false starts, the encroaching ashes, the crimes belly-high, the dead and the lies, I believe and still believe in mankind and the future. If the dumbos don't blow it away first.

BARBARA: Mankind's fine enough if you don't forget your hobnail boots. Father would've been proud of you, Irene.

IRENE: And Mother would've been proud of you and Kathy. You made it rich.

KATHERINE: Mother taught us there's only yourself in the world; try not to be a bastard if possible, but, above all, don't be poor.

IRENE: That was Mother, she liked to have her cake – and yours, too.

BARBARA: I often wonder what would've happened if she hadn't taken Kathy and me and left you with Father?

IRENE: She gave me up early. No, the real wonder is how those two ever came together in the first place.

BARBARA: She swore she was originally Tudor gentry and he was Polish nothing. She was descended from the Cecils, so she said. How could it ever have worked? She never told us why she married him. Probably based on a complete misunderstanding like most marriages.

KATHERINE: Wasn't he studying to be a doctor when they met?

IRENE: Yes, but he got interested in philosophy. He wasn't very practical because he always had that insatiable thirst for knowledge.

BARBARA: And Mother had this insatiable thirst for money. I know there are things money can't buy but they weren't the things Mother was ever interested in.

KATHERINE: She never forgave Father for ending up a teacher.

IRENE: Oh, but he was such a good one, even though he hated schools – 'stupid, bourgeois instruction for the poor!' He had such a passionate intelligence. It never stagnated or recoiled from an inquiry or conclusion. 'I only propose, never impose.' He'd say things you'd always remember.

BARBARA: 'Conger eels have no teeth but very hard gums.'

(*They laugh.*)

IRENE: 'Knowledge sucks, wisdom dribbles.' A session with
Father would send me scurrying round museums and
libraries, filling notebook after notebook.

KATHERINE: It just sent me scurrying round to dressmaker
after dressmaker, I'm afraid. That was never for you, Irene,
you'd get dizzy wearing high-heeled shoes. Barbie and I
must've had deeply shallow minds.

BARBARA: We took after Mother. The day war was declared,
she got into a taxi and had her hair washed. But she knew
the marriage market. Whatever happened, she never lost
the opportunity to display our wares to rich young men who
had even less in their pants than in their heads. Remember
Viscount Freddy August and Anthony Coombs-Bart? It's
no wonder before I found Ralph I went through three
husbands – oil, wheat and shipping. I took what they gave
me. That's all they had. Ralph was different. He looked
like the poet Byron and his grandmother made bird's nests.
He impressed Mother because his tailor was Kilgrove,
Busby and Hurt and they mounted his individual suit
pattern on the wall right next to the Prince of Wales. That
clinched it for Mother, she gave her approval. It didn't
matter, he was the love of my life. He was like the sun, a
joy to all my senses. I found him after such a long search. I
was always surprised you latched on to George so quickly,
Kath.

KATHERINE: George Gould had old money – that's the best
kind – money, like wine, needs time to mature and grow
generation to generation. Aged-in-the-wood money, settled
money, money in the blood. It's very easy to say 'yes' to a
merchant banker.

IRENE: George is also a noted ornithologist.

KATHERINE: How can I forget it, through glen and fell with the
Ring-tailed Orange Coot?

BARBARA: You can't live for or through others but I'm glad we
made Mother happy in the end. She had her diamonds and
her summer house in Rhodes. You know, Irene, when she

died, her room was full of artificial flowers. She loved them
because they were always in bloom and never had slugs.

IRENE: Father died happy, too. He wrote to me three weeks
before he collapsed that he was enjoying himself teaching in
Lagos . . . they needed him . . . dropped dead at noon . . .
A friend told me he had his ticket in his pocket and the sole
of his right shoe was tied with string. He always said it
didn't matter much how you died, so long as you laid down
your life for the oppressed. His way wasn't my way, too
gentle, but you can't live the revolutions of others. I believe
you have to yell 'open!' and break your fists against the
door – fists, heads, hearts broken, too, and why not? Why
not? Anything's better than acceptance . . . Give me a glass
of water, Kathy.

(KATHERINE *pours her a glass*.)

KATHERINE: Are you all right?

IRENE: Not really. I'd better take a pill . . . there they are . . .
(*She takes a pill and drinks*.) You know, it's good talking
together after all these years.

BARBARA: I used to miss Father, which was stupid. We didn't
see him for what – fifteen, twenty years? A postcard on our
birthdays – always. Yet I knew he was out there somewhere
and because he was, I wasn't alone.

IRENE: You had Mother.

BARBARA: Mother wasn't a person, more a way of life.

KATHERINE: I felt that, too. Perhaps if Father had turned up
I'd've just been embarrassed like I was with you that time,
Irene. But after all, you were notorious – 'Red Irene', the
Revolutionary Crosby Girl: the mad one. All those reports
from Spain, China, Cuba and the rest.

BARBARA: We were proudly ashamed of you, Irene, deep down.
But it was difficult. I lost count of the number of times your
name came up between soup and fish when we were out
dining with Lady Curzon. You made her shiver. She had a
chip on her shoulders. That's easy to understand, she had
plenty of wood higher up.

KATHERINE: You were a legend and Father was something of a

61

myth. George never met him, though he wanted to. As he got on so well with you, Irene, he thought he'd get on with Father. Father never risked it. I was grateful to him then, now I think I was wrong.

IRENE: Here we are, three old . . .

BARBARA: Oldish, Irene, oldish.

IRENE: Here we are, three oldish old ladies talking about our father as if he were only yesterday.

BARBARA: He is only yesterday. The days when we were all together – sisters together – they seem only yesterday. That last picnic, when we were living in the house near the esplanade of the old Dover Castle above the sea.

KATHERINE: The summer 'talkies' came in. Were those last years before the war ever real? . . . We were on a clifftop, lying on a blanket . . . It was full of dog's hair . . . that was Muldoon.

IRENE ⎫
        ⎬ : Poor Muldoon!
BARBARA ⎭

(*They laugh.*)

KATHERINE: The wasps kept dropping into the honey . . . fish paste sandwiches, strawberry jam and cherry cake. I've never eaten so well since and I've always eaten four-star.

BARBARA: Father made us lie on our backs and hold our breath. He said if we concentrated, we could feel the world turning . . . turning. I can still see the gulls and the fish breaking water and the sailing boats way out in the Channel.

IRENE: Shhh . . . shhh . . . we'll become rotten with memories . . .

BARBARA: Do you need anything, Irene?

IRENE: A new lease of life . . . new heart for old.

BARBARA: They'd never find one big enough for you, dear.

IRENE: Wasn't that the day Father decided to teach us 'The Internationale'? Oh, Mother's face . . . and that's more than fifty years gone . . . I'm sure that's the moment she decided to leave.

KATHERINE: (*Singing*) 'The people's flag is brightest red . . .

our martyred dead . . . so raise the scarlet banner high
within its shade we'll live and die . . .' I still remember.
Isn't it terrible? What would the Duchess have said if she'd
known?

BARBARA: Father was disappointed with us, wasn't he?

IRENE: He loved you and Katherine.

BARBARA: He wanted us to be more like you, Irene. But it was
much easier for you to set out to change the world.

IRENE: Easier?

BARBARA: We weren't built for revolutionary politics. We had
other needs. When I was young I had a body like a
limousine, now it's more like a burlap bag but then it was
quite something. It should've been, I ate like a dyspeptic
butterfly.

KATHERINE: We two were international beauties along with
Gladys Cooper.

IRENE: And I wasn't beautiful?

BARBARA: It wasn't that so much. You had a terrific intelligence
but you didn't try to hide it. We always loved you, Irene,
but in those days you had all the ease and grace of an iron
foundry.

KATHERINE: You were too serious.

IRENE: So I took up revolutionary politics because I was ugly
and charmless.

KATHERINE: Who said that, exactly?

IRENE: I couldn't fall in love with a man so I fell in love with
mankind.

BARBARA: You weren't ever too interested in personal
relationships, you said so yourself.

IRENE: I've always known it like a fox, that's what you thought
. . . ah! . . . the pain!

BARBARA: Don't work yourself up.

IRENE: You're saying I spent all my life fighting injustice and
cruelty because I'm a frustrated spinster?!

KATHERINE: Why do we have to shout when we meet? All we
said was you never married and never got a man for
yourself.

IRENE: You mean couldn't get?! . . . You'd better ask Ralph and George about that!

BARBARA: Do you need another pill? You're looking greyish.

KATHERINE: Ask George? What's my husband got to do with it?

BARBARA: Should I get a nurse? . . . What about Ralph?

IRENE: I had affairs with both of them . . . not simultaneously, of course.

KATHERINE: How can you say a thing like that in a public hospital?

IRENE: I can say it because it's true. No, the truth's just an excuse. I can say it because I'd like to get it off my chest after all these years, purge my soul. No, that's an excuse, too. I can say it because I'm in a rage . . . in pain . . . I'm lashing out, so duck! I've been a stirrer all my life. Oh, I'll be sorry in the morning . . . it's petty, it's mean, ignoble. Oh, but it's satisfying!

KATHERINE: I don't believe a word of it.

IRENE: You wouldn't. For sixty-nine years you've managed never to believe anything that was the least disturbing. You've always surrounded yourself with yourself, that's what's kept you young.

BARBARA: When was this supposed to have happened?

IRENE: With dear gone Ralph, it was a brief mad, glad adventure in the summer of '53. I was in Milan reporting on the steel strike for the *Socialist International*. We met by chance in a storm. It was a big city and I didn't want to be alone. And so began the joy of my life. Lying here now, old, who knows the why of it? He seemed so self-contained, so English. But that summer he came out of a storm and there was a storm inside him. We decided to commit suicide to stay together and he threw me down a flight of stairs when I changed my mind. I wept enough tears for him to refloat Moby Dick. Just personal, just personal . . . It couldn't've lasted, our politics were too far apart, our values so different . . . But for three weeks . . . the sweet pain of it still . . . a different sort of pain than this pain now . . . I left him early one Monday morning but he caught me at the platform with an engraved bracelet, a pre-packed lunch box and a red rose. I went to North Korea, he went to the Louis Quatorze hotel, Paris.

BARBARA: The Louis Quatorze . . . that was the year Eric and Susan went down with food poisoning . . . I think he had something important to tell me, I forget what it was now . . . We were on the terrace . . . I'm sure he mentioned a journey. A long time ago . . . The doctor came in and told us about the children in French. No use at all. Was that the time it happened?

KATHERINE: Who cares if it was or not? Ralph's dead. You can't saw sawdust. I mean, it's finished, over. George is still alive, more or less.

BARBARA: Stop thinking about yourself.

KATHERINE: Who else is going to think about me? What about you and George?

IRENE: That was different. A brief affair that lasted, a spring romance that went on till autumn. We were also on opposite sides of the world, to say nothing of the fence. We never saw each other for years but when we met it was like we'd never been apart. He's a comforting man.

KATHERINE: I know what he is. At least I thought I did.

IRENE: He used to read me to sleep from the *Book of British Birds*. 'The Snow Bunting is a stockily built bunting. In the male the whole wing is white, apart from black primaries and bastard wing.' I'd read extracts from Gramsci. 'The error of the intellectual consists in believing it is possible to *know* without understanding and especially without feeling and passion . . . history and politics cannot be made without passion, without this emotional bond between intellectuals and the people.'

KATHERINE: George only reads the *Financial Times*. He's a banker's banker.

IRENE: For you. For me he was an ornithologist. We both had to watch and wait.

KATHERINE: I don't believe it. I'll never believe it. And if it's true, I still won't believe it.

BARBARA: It's your damn Socialism! Share everything – who said you could share Ralph?

KATHERINE: Or George. There's not enough of him for one. I thought intellectuals were always supposed to be cold and calculating. You didn't ever fall into the trap of the personal you said. Now it turns out it's free love and passion and flesh and the devil.

BARBARA: It's all in the mind. You're just envious of us.

IRENE: I've never been envious. Ask Ralph.

BARBARA: I can't without a Ouija board. Ralph's dead, remember.

IRENE: Not for me.

KATHERINE: Well, I shall ask George and he'll tell me it's a pack of lies.

IRENE: If he does, I'll agree with him . . . all lies . . . old woman's lies . . . tired lies . . .

KATHERINE: Oh, that's really nasty. It means I'll never know for sure. This has come at a very bad time for me. I've had forty good married years with George but the bills from the beauty parlours get bigger every year. I think he's beginning to notice at last.

BARBARA: Don't cry, Kath, please. It's only effective when you're in your twenties.

IRENE: No, don't cry . . . I shouldn't've said anything . . . true or false . . . as I grow older I prefer fake politeness to sincere boorishess . . . The years pass and it gets harder . . . the struggle to change the world . . . Great rivers, why do you flow? Snowy mountains, how long will you last? . . . You only understand life backwards . . . A telephone pole is an edited tree, Father said . . . Tired . . . and I hurt . . . Did you know Hitler's socks kept falling down? . . . (*She sleeps.*)

KATHERINE: I don't care about Hitler's socks . . . Irene? Irene don't go to sleep now! This is important.

BARBARA: No, it isn't. She just wanted to get at us, that's all. Sisters get jealous of each other. We used to fight over who had the biggest slice of cherry cake . . .

KATHERINE: I've never known Irene to lie.

BARBARA: She's very ill. Drugged, too. And in pain. Irene and Ralph, it's absurd. Irene and George, never.

KATHERINE: You seem sure.

BARBARA: Not completely but pretty sure. Look at it with cool logic like Irene usually looked at a problem. Irene was never pretty and always intellectual. All her life she was a political revolutionary. Now, ask yourself one question – why should Ralph or George want her when they had us?

KATHERINE: That's so right. They had the best.

BARBARA: We must be very understanding with Irene. She is our sister and nothing's worked out for her: she's been very disappointed. As far as I can see, she's not had one successful revolution to her name. We've had it all, money, position, power, dined with kings. She's known only hard bread and hardship. She followed a dream and never caught it. Of course she's bitter.

KATHERINE: I won't say anything to George, it'd be too hurtful to him. I should know the truth about George and me after the experience of forty years together. Everything's fine. I feel it in my heart.

BARBARA: No, experience is in your fingers, in your head, never in your heart. I'm afraid the heart is inexperienced.

IRENE: (*Suddenly waking*) I knew a man who, when he got depressed, used to have his arms tattooed as a reminder of the danger of giving way to cruelty. It was very useful.

KATHERINE: Why aren't you sleeping?

IRENE: Why aren't you taller? Take no notice of what I said before, I was babbling.

BARBARA: We understand, dear. We've been far apart on most things for most of our lives but despite it all, we've always been sisters.

KATHERINE: Nothing can change that, not revolutions or revelations. The rest isn't important.

IRENE: I know what is important. Sometimes it seemed a crazy business to spend all my energies trying to save a world

which had no desire to be saved. But there you are . . . we
picked ourselves up after one escapade and tumbled straight
into the next . . . And so . . . and so . . . The important
thing is, I've had a happy life.

BARBARA: You have?

IRENE: Very. And you?

BARBARA: I don't know . . . yes.

KATHERINE: Yes . . . yes!

IRENE: That's good . . . I'm sleepy again . . . Don't go yet . . .
Sing me to sleep . . . we used to long ago in the old
nursery.

BARBARA: Sing what?

IRENE: (*Laughing*) What else? . . . (*Nostalgically sings lines
from 'Sisters' by Irving Berlin.* BARBARA *and* KATHERINE
join in, laughing.)

DANCING

*A dance studio. A cassette player on a piano plays music from
MacMillan's* Romeo and Juliet *whilst* SUSAN MICHELL *practises.*

SUSAN: (*To herself*) Beautiful . . . keep it beautiful . . . Dancing
is beautiful . . . If a thing doesn't dance, it doesn't exist for
me. I live in dance not in reality or reason. When I'm
dancing, I'm everything that moves . . . light, air, summer
wind . . . an island of grace in a graceless world . . .
yes . . .

(*A door opens behind her, Up Stage Centre and the misshapen,
hunchback figure of* MICHAEL PAULLEIN *enters and shuffles
menacingly towards her. She turns and screams in fright.*)

PAULLEIN: Awaa . . . awahh . . .

SUSAN: Michael? . . . Is that you?

PAULLEIN: Quasy . . . Quasy . . .

SUSAN: What're you doing in that black wig and the rest?

PAULLEIN: Quasy . . .

SUSAN: Quasy what?

PAULLEIN: Modo. Quasimodo. I'm understudying Quasimodo
in the ballet, *The Hunchback of Notre Dame*, next week.
Susan, how does the costume and everything look? The wig
. . . eyepatch . . . crippled arm and leg . . . and the *hump*!
Good, isn't it? I thought it up myself. It only has one
drawback as a ballet costume. I can't dance in it. (*He jumps
and spins unsteadily.*) See what happens . . . my hump keeps
slipping about. (*He jumps again.*) See . . . it's shifted. I
can't dance with a wandering hump, can I? I'll get it right.
I just wanted to give you a quick flash.

SUSAN: You gave me that.

PAULLEIN: (*Taking off his wig and eyepatch*) I'd better take some
of it off, right now. There'll be time for it later. But the
thing is, I want it to be completely authentic. As the ballet's
set in Paris, I wonder if I should dance it in French?

SUSAN: Don't worry about that stuff now, Michael, please.

71

She'll be here any minute. You know, this will be the first
Master Class Diane Kirby has taken since she retired five
years ago. Do you realize how lucky we are to be her first
pupils?

PAULLEIN: Lucky? I guess so. It's about time. We're the best
but usually the flawless go down and the faulty rise. The
trouble has always been I'm cursed with intelligence as well
as talent. Most ballet dancers would be in asylums if they
had brains.

SUSAN: I'm not intelligent, just nervous. And when I'm nervous
my body doesn't work. Diane Kirby was my idol, the first,
best and always.

PAULLEIN: She danced people! . . . Let's warm up.
(*They practise together.*)

SUSAN: I'll always be grateful for the beauty she showed me.
Without her . . . I was born handicapped – hyperactivity
and a severe case of asthma.

PAULLEIN: Snap! I had it, too. (*He draws breath loudly.*) *Haa-
haa-haa.*

SUSAN: Don't do that, it's infectious. Asthma made me a terror
as a kid. Once I painted the living room sick purple when
everybody was out. It got so bad, when I decided to run
away from home, my father actually packed my suitcase for
me. Then I was taken to see Diane Kirby dance *Romeo and
Juliet*. For the first time in my life I could breathe. I threw
away my inhaler and bought a pair of ballet shoes: I began
dancing.

PAULLEIN: My story – almost. There wasn't a day I didn't get
an attack. I felt like a blocked exhaust living in a drainpipe.
We didn't live in a slum, you understand, just a rubbishy
neighbourhood. My mother took me to dance classes
because she thought that sort of exercise might help my
asthma. And it did. I never had it again, except maybe
when I think of all those defective Russian dancers coming
over here to take our places. I find it hard to breathe when
Baryshnikov and his hordes're at the gates. The kids at
school thought I was a fairy, taking on dancing classes. I

soon put a stop to that.

SUSAN: How?

PAULLEIN: I beat up the little creeps. Actually, I'd've had an easier career if I had been a fairy, as they called it. The international homosexual conspiracy to dominate the ballet in London, New York and Paris makes the Comintern look like a touring company of *The Student Prince*. Missed opportunity there. When I took up jazz dancing, the kids' attitude changed. They thought I was cool. I'd've gone down that jazz road if I hadn't seen Diane Kirby dance. After that glimpse of perfection, all I wanted was the pure beauty of classical ballet. I still do despite all the disappointment and pain.

SUSAN: No pliés without pain. Every night I rub aspirin on my feet, wrap them in bandages, then a sock, then a heating pad. Nothing's going to stand in my way, not pain or pleasure. Look at Anna Dupleiss. She was the most promising dancer of my year. Now she's expecting.

PAULLEIN: Who?

SUSAN: A baby.

PAULLEIN: Whatever got into her?

SUSAN: Who knows? Whatever it was, it's done for her now. Terrible not to be able to dance. It's the only thing between us and real life. I have to make it to the top.

PAULLEIN: Me, too. We're alike. You know, the higher I rise the easier I breathe.

SUSAN: The air's beautiful up there with the stars. Diane Kirby knows and she should help us. She was unique. She made other ballerinas look like middle-aged truck drivers.

PAULLEIN: She was airy stuff.

(*The door opens and* DIANE KIRBY *comes in, crosses to the piano and puts her shopping bag down on top of it.*)

SUSAN: Miss Kirby . . .

DIANE: (*Croaking*) A little lower.

PAULLEIN: Lower?

DIANE: Voice . . . voice . . .

SUSAN: Oh . . . (*Low*) yes . . .

PAULLEIN: (*Low*) I'm Michael Paullein and this is Susan Michell.

SUSAN: (*Low*) This is a great honour, Miss . . .

DIANE: Yes, dear . . . Why don't you continue with what you were doing whilst I unpack my bag?

PAULLEIN: Of course . . . Susan . . .

(PAULLEIN *turns away to escort* SUSAN *to the middle of the studio.*)

DIANE: Arrrr! He's got a bleeding great goitre on his arse!

PAULLEIN: Who? Who?

DIANE: You! You! Twist round – see!

PAULLEIN: (*Twisting round*) Oh, that's just my wandering Quasimodo hump. It must've slipped down. Sorry.

SUSAN: It's just part of a costume he was trying out, Miss Kirby.

DIANE: Oh, that's a relief. I thought I was seeing little green 'uns again.

PAULLEIN: It's all right. I'll take it off . . . when I can find it . . . Ahh, here it is. (*He takes off his hump.*)

DIANE: That's quite a sight this early in the morning. (*She takes a six-pack of beer from her bag.*) The six-pack of beer is the greatest invention since sliced bread. You drink one can and you know you've got five left. Very comforting . . . (*She switches off the cassette player.*) It's too early for me to listen to you dance, when I'm suffering from the wrath of grapes – that's a hangover, dearies, a hangover. I've got two dozen beer and gin gnomes folk-dancing in my head. (*She opens a can of beer.*) Want one?

SUSAN: No thank you.

PAULLEIN: No.

DIANE: (*Drinking*) I know you two can dance. I saw you six months ago at the Ballet Gala. Beautiful . . . flawless . . . you know the 'how' of it but what about the 'what' of it and the 'why' of it? To find out the 'what' and 'why' we have to talk. Come closer, round the piano here.

(PAULLEIN *and* SUSAN *join her by the piano. Whilst she leans against it, they sit on the floor in front of her.*)

DIANE: You ask questions. I can tell you things that are
    important. I've danced my time.

SUSAN: There is one question I've always wanted to ask you.
    You had the ballet world at your feet. Balanchine and all
    the other great choreographers wanted you and you had
    years of dance left. Yet you left it . . . Why?

PAULLEIN: I just hope I'll be intelligent enough to know when
    to leave it. Like Garbo you left when you were on top. You
    left beautiful memories and nobody got nervous for you,
    Miss Kirby.

DIANE: Booze. I left because of booze and the other thing. I was
    hitting the hot sauce hard. And I didn't want to do any
    more tours. Have you any idea what that's like? Sometimes
    a different city every day. Mornings I'd wake up and I
    didn't know the name of the hotel, city or stud sleeping
    next to me. That was when I was lucky. Usually I slept
    alone. I'd work three hours before lunch – steak and salad
    for protein. Then two hours' rest in a chalk circle on the
    floor, storing up psychic energy, thinking of Raphael,
    Archangel of Air. Make a note, the circle's useful as a
    barrier against negative influences. Then a two-hour private
    warm-up at the theatre. Put on make-up and costume, go
    out onstage before curtain-up to check the spacing of the
    scenery and cracks in the floor. Then performance,
    applause, airport, flight and waking up in another unknown
    grot-town.

SUSAN: That could easily make you fall out of love with
    dancing.

DIANE: I fell out of love with dancers. Always be on your toes
    against them, children. They're everywhere. And they're
    gunning for you. Envy never sleeps. (*She opens another can
    of beer and drinks.*)

SUSAN: But aren't they your fellow artists, partners helping you
    create a world of everlasting beauty?

DIANE: I'll tell you about partners and everlasting beauty! They
    drove me out. Take notes, take notes! It's straight from the
    horse's, one hundred per cent proof. It started one night. I

was on pointe for the Black Swan variation. That's when I heard it. It was quite soft at first, but long drawn out and still deadly. It was aimed at me. I knew it could only be my partner, Alexi Tarkovsky.

PAULLEIN: Tarkovsky. I believe it, whatever it is. He's another one with snow on his ballet shoes.

DIANE: He was standing directly behind me when he did it again – more confidently this time.

SUSAN: What did he do, Miss?

DIANE: Broke wind.

SUSAN: Broke what?

DIANE: Wind. Not once but again and again – it was horrifying . . . *brrr* . . . *brrr* . . . It had to be Tarkovsky, it was always his easiest means of communication . . . *brrrrr* . . . He wanted to blow me off balance if he could . . . *brrr* . . . *brrr* I staggered but I didn't fall – never that – years of training . . . I completed my variations under another devastating volley . . . *brrr* . . . *brrr* . . . *brrr* . . . When I finally turned and faced my partner, he didn't betray himself; not a flicker. Those damn Russian faces! But the chorus knew. Those bitches sniggering away on their ballooney legs; they knew. It happened the next night and the next . . . *brrr* . . . *brrr* . . . No wonder I took to drink. Nobody said anything. They didn't have to . . . *brrr* . . . *brrrr*. I finally broke a lampstand on Tarkovsky's skull backstage during a performance of *Giselle*. He hardly noticed he's so thick there, but I found myself in my local Psychiatric Hospital, where malpractice is almost a thing of the past. What did they know about the profession? Not an Equity member amongst them. How could they know that dancing in a top ballet company is like dancing in a tank of piranha fish.

SUSAN: (*Coughing*) Is it true? Is it like that at the top?

DIANE: The higher the tighter the noose. The top is the pits.

PAULLEIN: It is true that no civilian has any concept of the Borgia-like intrigue rampant in your average ballet. We feel it too, Miss Kirby.

DIANE: Call me Diane. Remember, a ballet dancer's life is short but there's always someone ready to make it shorter, partners, colleagues, friends – friends're the worst. Take notes! I know, look how I ended up. My spot went black. I tried dozens of clinics to cure my drinking and paranoia, so-called. I even found myself in California taking a therapy called crotch-eyeballing. That's where the victim – I mean, the patient – lies down with his or her legs apart and the rest of us would stare at the exposed genitalia. Not a pretty sight. Ugh. (*She shudders and drinks.*)

SUSAN: But did it help?

DIANE: Yes, it did. It made me see I was sane and the doctors mad. My paranoia was no sick dream. I'd been blown out. The *brrr*, *brrrs* were real. And once I faced the fact I was an alcoholic, I could enjoy my drinking. I'm not as big a fool as I used to be, I've dieted. Isn't it about time you two started dancing?

PAULLEIN: Yes!

SUSAN: Please!

(*The two eagerly scramble up from the floor.*)

DIANE: When you dance, whole rooms should become bigger. We'll take *Romeo and Juliet*. When I danced Juliet, I had skin like yours, Susan, as clear and transparent as a débutante's. People marvelled at my skin. Many's the time I've walked down the Fulham Road and heard people say, 'There she goes. I marvel at her skin, it's as clear and transparent as a débutante's.' Michael O'Leary, you've got a great pair of jugs on you.

PAULLEIN: (*Coughing*) What? Jugs? . . . Oh, yes, thanks. Shouldn't we dance?

DIANE: Yes, but dance, people. People, I said, people. When I first danced Juliet I knew people. I was young but I was already married to Donald Gough-Walker. He was earmarked as a future Minister of Arts. Well, he did have one of the biggest collections of banknotes in the country. He was older than me, but it's better for a man to marry a young girl and satisfy her curiosity than marry a widow and disappoint her. (*She opens another can.*) Remember that's

important for your dancing. Why aren't you taking notes?!
Donald and me split up over religion. He was a strict
Anglican and I was an atheist. He couldn't stand it when we
made love and I kept saying, 'Oh my non-existent Supreme
Being!' You've got *thighs*, Michael lad! I feel like feeling
you up.

PAULLEIN: Feeling me . . . where?!

DIANE: Up! Up! We're wasting time. Why aren't you dancing?!

SUSAN: You haven't given us a chance!

DIANE: Because there's more to dancing than just moving your
feet. You've got to've lived before you can dance. I
divorced Donald before I was twenty-two – I can recom-
mend Chattles, Wattles and Swift as the best divorce
lawyers in town. If I hadn't married again, I could've lived
comfortably on the bounty from the mutiny – that's
alimony, dearies, alimony. Actually, I married three more
times if you count the rock singer. I was foolish like Juliet.
Michael O'Shea, have you got a cigarette, I need my daily
dose of death.

PAULLEIN: No . . . no, I don't smoke. What about . . . ?

DIANE: Girlie! Girlie!

SUSAN: What?!

DIANE: Juliet isn't your wilting English rose type – oh no. No.
She's not second hand but she's a hot one. (*She rushes over
and switches on the cassette tape of* Romeo and Juliet *Act III
Scenes 1 and 2*.) This is the part where Juliet's family try to
force her to marry Paris. She doesn't love Paris – who does
in August? So they throw her to the ground. (*She crashes
down*.) Ah! Ah! Juliet cries. (*She sobs*.) I could always do
that part well enough, well enough. Then Juliet sees
Romeo's cloak. (*She scrambles up*.) Is that your coat,
Michael O'Day? That'll do. (*She staggers over and picks up
Michael's coat*.) She caresses her face with it, her body,
between her legs . . . tears at it in her grief. (*There is a
ripping sound*.) Ooh . . . Sorry.

PAULLEIN: That's my coat, Miss Kirby!

DIANE: Diane I insist. Diane. Juliet sits on the bed and thinks.

78

Thinks . . . you've got to look as though you're thinking.
That's always hard for dancers. I've seen better heads on
glasses of beer.

SUSAN: (*Gasping*) Thinking? Thinking about what?

DIANE: Screwing. (*She opens another can of beer.*) That's what I
thought about before I was blown away and that's what
Juliet thought about. Juliet sees Friar Lawrence and falls at
his feet. Michael Flynn, stand there and I'll fall at your feet.
(*She rushes across and collapses at* PAULLEIN's *feet.*)

PAULLEIN: Careful . . .

DIANE: Father Lawrence! Help me, Father Lawrence, help me
have a good screw tonight!

PAULLEIN: Please let go of my legs.

DIANE: (*Clinging to him*) No, I want them. I want them. Listen
children, every minute of the day one hundred thousand
men and women die, plop, just like that. Every minute, so
screw it. Humping and screwing is the thought to hold. I
say screw dancing when you could be screwing, like Juliet.
(*She staggers up, holding on to* PAULLEIN.)

PAULLEIN: You're ripping my tights!

SUSAN: (*Gasping*) It's all so ugly.

(DIANE *crosses, switches off the cassette player and opens
another can.*)

DIANE: It's real, lassie. The world's real and dancing's no
protection. Don't turn your head away. Look here at yours
truly. I'm living in Leighton Buzzard with five weeks' dirty
washing and not a biscuit in the house that isn't middle-
aged.

SUSAN: (*Gasping*) *Haa haa.* I don't want to know that.

PAULLEIN: (*Gasping*) Susan, please calm down. Ha . . . remember you said how asthma's contagious.

SUSAN: (*Gasping*) It's *her*.

DIANE: Of course it's me and mine. I'm jus' giving you fair
warning, it'll happen to you one day. You'll be at the top,
dancing on air, at the Met or whatever; chandeliers,
evening dresses and a thousand expensive eyes s'watching
and you'll hear behind you soft . . . oh, so soft . . . *brrr*

... *brrr* ... It's the last trumpet. *Brrr* ... maybe you'll turn to drink, soft drugs or softer thighs but you won't shut it out. It's the sound of the world blowing in.

(SUSAN *and* PAULLEIN *gasp loudly for breath. Both have asthma attacks.*)

SUSAN: (*Gasping*) *Haaa . . . haaa . . .* ugly . . . ugly *haaa . . .*

PAULLEIN: (*Gasping*) *Haaa . . .* why are you . . . telling . . . *haaa . . .* us this stuff . . .

DIANE: It's my job. Got to teach you not to dance through your life blind. I have to teach now, y'see. I'm broke. So if this class goes well, I'll get others.

SUSAN: (*Gasping*) *Haaa aaa . . .* others?!

DIANE: You two've talked enough. 'Stime you danced . . . dance!

PAULLEIN: (*Gasping*) Miss Kirby, I don't know if you've noticed but we're both having asthma attacks . . . *haaa.*

DIANE: And I'm so pissed my back teeth are floating. So? So? So? We're the walking wounded. Dancing isn't just for summer days, it's a winter sport too. Art isn't a diversion, it's got to teach us to face the fact that life doesn't end well. On your toes and dance. (*She switches on the cassette player to the Balcony Scene of* Romeo and Juliet *Act I Scene 6.*)

PAULLEIN: (*Gasping*) You're mad *haa . . . haa . . . haa . . .*

SUSAN: (*Gasping*) How can we dance, we can't . . . breathe *haaa haaaa.*

(DIANE *staggers over to them and starts pulling them to their feet.*)

DIANE: That's good. Use it. Juliet and her Romeo felt like you're feeling. On your feet – up! Up! You're gasping for breath like they're gasping for each other. Up! You're suffocating from lack of air, they're suffocating from lack of love. They're cripples like you. You need love and air. It's'matter of life and death in that order. On your feet! On your feet. Look truth in the face and dance.

(SUSAN *and* PAULLEIN *are doubled up with the effort of trying to breathe.*)

SUSAN: (*Gasping*) Can't . . .

PAULLEIN: (*Gasping*) No . . .

DIANE: Yes . . . Hold her in the penchée . . . don't look at the
floor . . . look at each other . . . arabesque pas de bourrée
. . . you look geriatric . . . good dancers dance well every
day . . . developé . . . developé . . .you don't have a hope
in hell of getting through this if you let your backside
spread . . .

(*Gradually* SUSAN *and* PAULLEIN *begin to dance as their
coughing and gaspings die away.*)

Dance as if you're dancing on the edge of eternity . . .
without lies . . . that's better . . . that's right . . . that's it!
. . . It's not flawless, it's *good* . . . now you're dancing
Romeo and Juliet dancing . . . you're dancing the pain and
the passion of it at last . . . don't you see, if you dance the
truth you always come away with something? . . . Dance,
damn you . . . dance . . .

(*She slumps to the floor as* SUSAN *and* PAULLEIN *continue
dancing with increasing confidence and vigour as the music
swells up.*)

THE PERFECT PAIR

Darkness. A woman is heard drunkenly singing 'Auld Lang Syne.'
'Should auld acquaintance be forgot and never brought to min'? Should
auld acquaintance be forgot, and days o' auld lang syne? For auld lang
syne, my dear, for auld lang syne, we'll tak' a cup o' kindness . . .' She
is cut off in mid-note with a gurgle. Two men are heard giggling in
drunken glee. Lights up on a room, Logs Lodging House, Tanners
Close, Edinburgh, 1828. BURKE *and* HARE *stagger in drunkenly Up*
Stage Centre, with a body and dump it on the bed. Their speech is
bizarre: a mixture of Scottish words with an Irish accent.

HARE: Och ai', Mr Burke, I loved that woman's voice except for
    twa things – my ears. She made 'em dirl and ring like mad.
    Lookee, her mouth's sa big she could sing a duet with
    herself.

BURKE: That's young Mary Paterson we've gaffed, Mr Hare.
    Nine o'clock on a frosty morning, fishwives skirling
    'Roug-a-rug, worstling herrings!' and we've got fresh meat
    on the hoof. She'll fetch fourteen pounds minimum, from
    our friend Professor of Anatomy, Dr Knox, 10 Surgeon's
    Square. Best prices offered for fresh meat! She'll be on
    display on the operating table afor eager students within an
    hour of delivery: then cut, sliced and opened. Only in
    Edinburgh, 1828, could two late Irishmen like ourselves
    rise and flourish by such means. Give us a wee dram.
    (A bottle is passed over and they sing to the tune of 'Mr
    Gallacher & Mr Sheen'.)

HARE: (*Singing*) 'Oh, Mr Burke.'

BURKE: (*Singing*) 'Yes, Mr Hare?'

HARE: (*Singing*) 'What is that corpse doing on the floor? Surely
    it's against the law. To pile up corpses by the score. So will
    you tell me what it's really for?'

BURKE: (*Singing*) 'Oh, Mr Hare.'

HARE: (*Singing*) 'Yes, Mr Burke?'

BURKE: (*Singing*) 'Now to my explanation you must duly heed.

It is by this bright and splendid deed. We make a profit and
fill a need.'

HARE: (*Singing*) 'Oh, it's business, Mr B.'

BURKE: (*Singing*) 'Exactly, Mr Hare.'

(*They roar with laughter and continue drinking.*)

Auld beadit, auld lang syne, auld mon'd, auld father, auld
world. Do you ken those are true Scottish words I've just
learnt? I'll learn more till they won't know me from a
native, och ai'. I dinnae have one true Scottish word when I
left the arsehole of the world – County Tyrone, Ireland,
1818.

HARE: Your memory's a marvel, Mr Burke. I dinnae ken when
I left Ireland's soggy shore. Even yesterday slips out from
under.

BURKE: I remember exactly. Born 1792, schooled in the
Presbyterian Church school in Orrey. I learnt about Hell
there, Mr Hare. Not the Pope's Hell, Calvin's Hell. When
God sent a sinner plunging doon into everlasting hellfire,
the sinner screamed, 'But I didnae ken, Lord!' And the
Lord roared back, 'Well, you ken the noo!' Always certain
I'd be more than a nochting spud farmer like ma auld
father. It's why I tried sa many different jobs – Jack of all –
baking, weaving, soldiering and marriage. I left a wife and
three bairns back in the Emerald Green.

HARE: What a memory the man has!

BURKE: Ma auld father wouldn't give me a plot of land, so I
knocked him doon and took the ferry ta Glasgow.
Twenty-six years auld and eager, wasn't I? Pick and
shovelled on the Union Canal with ma sweet doxy Helen
McDougal, then clouted old shoes, 'Cobbler, cobbler –
bring me yer auld shoes!' I've had a lot ta do with old
clothes all ma life: second-hand stuff. All that time I was
just waiting fer ma time.

HARE: Our time, Mr B. *Awaaa.* I'm a mangy wolf howling for
the moon. I cannae remember like you but I left auld
Ireland sometime and worked for the Union Canal, too.
Had ta grub it in the waesome backlands of Glasgow, years.

86

But I had schemes ta make my fortune. There was ma
Scottish Ventilating Hat. Never told you that one. It was a
tartan top hat with a movable crown. I just used a tube ta
stick a valve ta a rubber bulb. You squeezed the bulb and
the valve lifted up the top hat – *bing, bing* – open and shut.
It stopped yer head from overheating at a stroke. It
could've save thousands from falling on the floor with fits.
They dinnae listen. I was doon but then I got sankie –
that's lucky, Mr Burke, lucky! The landlord of this street
lodging fell awa dead and his scranky fey queen widow took
a fancy ta me. I'm a fancy man when I put ma mind ta it.
(*He capers around.*) So I moved in with scranky queen
Maggie Laird; she's got a sharp tongue on her but seven
lodging rooms takes the edge off it. With capital, I could
turn this seven-room rat-trap into the most elegant brothel
in Edinburgh – with capital. That was but a dream. Then
auld Douglas died on us.

BURKE: November 29th 1827. We were twa sankie folk that
day.

HARE: I dinnae think so when I shouted, 'He's dead and he still
owes three pounds rent fer his lodging. How am I going ta
collect? Auld Douglas is bare, he's owning nothing I can
turn into hard cash . . . 'cept his body!' I had the idea first,
Mr Burke, I had the idea first.

BURKE: And I turned it into a paying business. We're a
twasome. Like meat and potatoes, belt and braces . . .

HARE: Soap and water, love and kisses . . .

BURKE: Black and Tan, Pearl and Dean . . .

HARE: Olsen and Johnson, Burke and Hare . . .

BURKE:(*Singing*) 'I don't know where I'm going.'

HARE: (*Singing*) 'Just as long as I'm with you.'

BURKE ⎱
HARE ⎰ : (*Singing*) 'Put it there pal
                Put it there.'

BURKE: (*Singing*) 'Old Scotland's full of policemen but we have
made them laughing stocks. The men are full of whisky and
the prisons have no locks.'

HARE: (*Singing*) 'You'll shock the wealthy hostesses when you turn up with no socks.'

BURKE ⎫
HARE ⎭ : (*Singing*) 'We make a perfect pair
                      Put it there.'

BURKE: (*Singing*) 'My colleague.'

HARE: (*Singing*) 'My crony.'

BURKE: (*Singing*) 'My cohort.'

HARE: (*Singing*) 'My friend.'

BURKE: (*Singing*) 'Companion, confederate, chumps to the end.'

HARE: (*Singing*) 'Like meat and potatoes.'

BURKE: (*Singing*) 'Or salt and tomatoes.'

BURKE ⎫
HARE ⎭ : (*Singing*) 'Boy what a blend
                      Don't put it in the papers
                      Don't leave it in the air
                      Don't keep it on the shelf
                      Put it there!'

(*They shake hands.*)

BURKE: Supply and demand, Mr Hare. Supply and demand. The medical schools need bodies fer their experiments. Cannae get 'em. If they could there'd be na demand fer our services. Presbyterians believe in the resurrection of the dead and if there's no body, no resurrection. So rich and poor alike guard them that's awa dead from the Snatchers, the Snatchers. And the demand grows and prices rise. (HARE *jumps up and down.*)

HARE: Seven pounds, ten shillings fer auld Douglas, seven pounds, ten shillings. Most people're worth more dead than alive.

BURKE: And what came next was ma idea, Mr Hare. Ma idea, ta go into the manufacturing end of the business and accelerate natural wastage. Remember Joseph the mumbling miller, the hard dier till I burked him: a pillow pressed tight over his face and he was with them that's awa.

HARE: Your idea, Mr Burke. If I had a hat, I'd take it off ta you. I held Joseph's legs when he struggled but it was your idea.

BURKE: My Lord Provost, Ladies and Gentlemen, ma partner and me are indeed honoured ta be asked ta speak ta the worthies of this great city. The firm of Burke and Hare . . .

HARE: I love the sound of that, Burke and Hare.

BURKE: Burke and Hare are always looking ta improve the efficiency of their business. Our success is due ta improvements in the vital areas of cost and production. The use of guns, axes, knives and iron bars is too expensive and leaves marks. Our customers dinnae like that. The fruit must be unblemished. But see here . . . a simple linen face-mask, filled with warm tar, clamped smartly over the victim's face . . .

HARE: (*Gurgling*) *Awaa arrrggg.*

BURKE: You took the words out of my mouth, *awaa arrrggg.* They cannae shout or breathe. They're killed without a bruise on 'em. We're certain this is the cheapest means of manufacturing corpses. It'd bring us great prestige if it were more generally known but Snatching is a secret community service. Like lawyers, we're not allowed ta advertise. Besides, if our services were known, it might lead ta unwelcome competition. Our competitors would flood into the manufacturing end of the market, once they discovered how easy it was.

HARE: Let 'em keep digging in graveyards, shovelling up the dead: it's the dirty end of the business.

BURKE: We, gentlemen, will continue ta carry on our business in the streets of this fair city. And we'll continue ta provide a discreet, reliable, personal service ta medical science. I thank you.

HARE: Mr B., Mr B., it seems ta me we're on the way ta being successful. At the start we sold two corpses every three months. Na' it's two corpses every three weeks and expanding. Till you turned off the tap. No more meat fer Dr Knox, you said. Why's that?

BURKE: Economics, Mr Hare. Friend Knox is desperate fer fresh corpses. We provide the best. If we cut off his supply temporarily, he'll ha'e ta come round ta our price.

HARE: You've a head on your shoulders. Mr Burke, as we plan ta expand, shouldn't we take on extra help?

BURKE: Risky. We dinnae want jus' any bairn. Difficult. He'd have ta have the right qualifications. He'd have ta be poor like us – well, that's easy. Poor and desperate ta better himself and not caring much how, like us – well, that's easy, too. But he'd have to have a strong stomach, keen eye, solid temperament. But, like us, he'd have ta have experience in second-hand goods – that's important.

HARE: I ken you were in old boots and I tinkered old pots and pans once but why's it important fer Snatching?

BURKE: Best training there is. Nocht like the fraggedy world of second-hand goods ta get a man inta the right frame of mind fer business. The system's got false bottoms, everything in it has twa values; everything bought and used up loses its value ta its owner. But it's still valuable ta somebody else lower doon – it sinks. Our bodies, too. They die, moulder, used up goods but they're still of value ta those in the know. People like us, used to dealing in second-hand goods: second-hand lives know how ta deal with second-hand bodies.

HARE: We've grown hard having ta haggle ta live, cheating, fighting, skinning down ta the bone.

BURKE: We're perfect fer this killing business. There's few who'd be so well qualified. So fer the time being, we'll have ta carry the burden, Mr Hare, sharing the work.

HARE: And the profits.

(*They laugh. There is a knock on the door.*)

DR KNOX'S VOICE: Burke . . . Hare . . . It's Dr Knox.

HARE: Should we cover up the body, Mr B?

BURKE: No, leave it on display. It'll be a good selling point . . . Come in, Doctor!

(DR KNOX *enters.*)

A wee, wee dram, Doctor?

DR KNOX: Damn your dram, Bum-belch! You've forced me ta visit you in this scunnersome stink-hole, called a lodging

house. They say it's got hot and cold running dirt in every
room. I believe it. Where're you and that nimple fyking
partner of yours been hiding? You promised you'd be a
reliable source of supplies . . . (*He notices the body on the bed
for the first time.*) Och ai, I'm sorry, I dinnae see the young
lady asleep.

BURKE: Lady?

DR KNOX: On the bed there, man.

HARE: Och, that's no lady, that's not even my wife.

BURKE: And she's noo asleep. Cannae yer see, Doctor, she's
dead.

DR KNOX: Dead . . . Dead? . . . Is she *mine*?!

BURKE: If the price is right.

DR KNOX: Top money fer top merchandise. Ten pounds. Cash.

BURKE: Eighteen.

DR KNOX: Eighteen! That's nearly double. So, that's why you
cut off the meat – ta jake up the price. It's cheating,
blackmailing, immoral . . .

BURKE: That's right, Doctor, it's business. But before you start
a-wailing, examine the quality of the carcass.

HARE: Young, fresh and healthy. No rubbish.

DR KNOX: I'll grant she looks in fair condition . . . wait . . .
dinnae I know this woman? I recognize her laying down.
That's the prostitute . . . the one with the daughter who's
awa' in the head . . . this is Mary . . . Mary . . .

BURKE: Paterson. Yes, anything wrong, Doctor?

HARE: Whores die too, they dooo, they dooo.

DR KNOX: Pretty Mary Paterson. This'll be a shock ta some of
ma students, meeting her again. They often used her
professional services when she was alive.

HARE: It'll be a lesson ta 'em, Doctor Knox. They cannae
always be slicing up strangers.

DR KNOX: Good point. It'll help eliminate any lingering touches
of sentiment, cutting into loving flesh.

BURKE: I thought fer a moment you were casting a first stone,
Doctor, that you had a prejudice against whores on your
dissecting table.

DR KNOX: That's enough! Hold your tongue.

HARE: (*Holding his tongue*) I aaa wooo ooodd . . . There, I held it, Doctor. Though I don't see . . .

DR KNOX: Syphilitic clown! I've fought all my life against prejudice of any kind – still fighting. Alive or dead, I make no distinction, race, colour, creed, all one under ma healing knife. Bring me yer tired, old, diseased, dispossessed, and I'll make use of those who've been useless all their lives!

HARE: Hallelujah! Hallelujah!

DR KNOX: Scientists cannae be prejudiced. They are seekers of truth. Truth is an activity and our discoveries are records of stages in the search fer truth. We're not interested in those discoveries as such, only in the search and we cannae be deflected by such encumbrances as petty prejudices. Have you any idea how Mistress Paterson came to die?

BURKE: From want of breath. But I'm no doctor, Doctor. She came here yesterday evening, ginned to the gills. In the middle of the night she was heard choking.

HARE: *Urrrgh . . . arrrgghh . . . ur!*

DR KNOX: Choked on her own vomit, I shouldn't wonder.

BURKE: I shouldnae wonder. We found her this morning, awa' dead.

DR KNOX: I'll have that dram the noo . . .

    (HARE *picks up a glass.*)

That glass is dirty Hare.

    (HARE *takes out a rag.*)

Don't clean it with that snotty rag, man. Give it ta me. Not the rag – the glass!

    (HARE *gives him the glass.* DR KNOX *cleans it with his own silk handkerchief.*)

HARE: Is that a silk handkerchief, Doctor? Best silk fer the best snouts eh, Doctor? Silk's what I call *class*, Doctor.

DR KNOX: I've earned it. (*He holds out his glass.*) Pour . . .

    (HARE *pours him a drink.*)

Enough.

    (DR KNOX *drinks.*)

BURKE: Silk handkerchiefs is living. We're not against it, we just want our share. It's what we deserve.

DR KNOX: If you twa got what you deserved, you'd starve ta death. Thanks ta the Law I'm forced ta keep company with the likes of you. The Law, the Law, it burkes the glory of Scottish medicine. There are easy ways fer 'em ta provide corpses fer us legal. But they're too douf-stupid ta think how.

BURKE: So you need the firm of Mr Burke and Mr Hare ta remind 'em of their duty.

HARE: Just twa merry, mad fellows doing their bit fer their adopted land – Scotland for ever and a day.

DR KNOX: It's because of Scotland and Scotland's stupidity I have ta seek the services of twa louse-ridden crottles called Burke and Hare. Another dram of barley-bree.
(*They pour him another drink.*)

HARE: Why do we let him speak ta us like that, Mr Burke?

BURKE: Because he has muckle money, Mr Hare. That's the sanction fer all abuses. But pay no heed ta it, laddie. It's the good Doctor's wee wounded pride. Mighty Scottish brains, mind's glory, need us twa chitterin' Irish-Scotty blathers ta carry their dirt.

DR KNOX: I dinnae need you, science does. It's all fer science. Science is what saves me from myself, nocht'll save you twa from being kilted in a tippet.

BURKE: What's that?

DR KNOX: Hanged, man.

BURKE: Kilted in a tippet . . . Never. We're untouchable. Business'll save us as science saves you. It's all fer business. There's no evidence ever of Snatching. The evidence has been sold, in the line of business and now destroyed by your science: cut, saw, slash, chopped into pieces.

HARE: Ta get ta us, they must go through you, good Doctor. If you was brought ta judgement, it'd show up all your baillies, provosts, judges and doctors as fine canting hypocrites: crack Church and State.

BURKE: This is 1828, Doctor. The country's changing and any man who cannae see it is blind. It's a new age, a 'making' age and we'll crow it, as safe as you, atop our dunghill.

HARE: Cock-a-doodle-do! Cock-a-doodle-do!

DR KNOX: Only half as safe as me because there's twa of you. Twa mouths, not one ta blather yer way ta perdition.

HARE } : Cock-a-doodle do!
BURKE }

DR KNOX: Snatching up corpses has got too easy, yer dizzy with how easy it is.

(HARE *capers around*.)

HARE: Oh, it is! It is!

BURKE: So how will it ever end, Doctor?

DR KNOX: You'll end it. Out of madness. One of you'll turn Judas.

BURKE: Fer thirty pieces of silver. I was only asking eighteen, Doctor, eighteen.

DR KNOX: You won't be Judas, Burke. You're too much of a betrayer. No one will trust you ta honour your word as a betrayer: they'll expect you ta go back on it. But Hare is mad enough ta be loyal to a Judas oath. If he says he'll betray you, he'll betray you.

HARE: I would. I would. Man of my word. Mr Burke knows that.

BURKE: It's the barley-bree talking. Ease up a dram, Mr Hare.

DR KNOX: You heard. So heed my warning. I dinnae care if you end with prison rot, torn ta pieces by the mob or dangle kilted in the wind, but I must have my carcasses. I'm insatiable. It's true, I need you ta go truffle-hunting, ta snout out where the best beef lies. And ta do that, you must stay clear of retribution. Otherwise, some Snatcher'll be digging up your carcasses fer ma table.

HARE: Oh, dig-dig-dig-dig. Dig fer yer supper. Sweet Mary Paterson, you ken just how we dug you, lassie. Before, you only felt a man's hot culls in your flesh, now you'll feel his cold knife. 'Oh, Mary, Mary, how does your garden grow?' We know how, Mary. We know everything. So does the good Doctor. He knows and dinnae want ta know: knowing and not knowing, like so many. Dinnae ken how we dood it, Doctor?

DR KNOX: I know too much already. That's why the medical establishment hates me.

BURKE: They're not the only ones, Doctor. But you dinnae know the half of it. It's time you knew all of it. You see, Doctor, it's more than just Snatching.

HARE: More, much more.

DR KNOX: I don't wish ta know that!

(BURKE *and* HARE *move towards him.*)

BURKE ⎫
HARE ⎭ : You'll know! We're telling!

DR KNOX: Gentlemen, one thing I already know, I'm going ta give you twa an exclusive contract.

(BURKE *and* HARE *stop.*)

BURKE: Contract?

DR KNOX: Verbal, of course. But binding fer all that. Its ta supply me with carcasses. I'll take all you can deliver. Eighteen pounds, adult male or female, ten fer a child, subject ta a six month revision. I'll deal only with you.

BURKE: Contract . . . that's recognized business practice. We appreciate this, Doctor. All we ask is ta be treated like respectable businessmen.

HARE: Appreciate.

BURKE: Sober up, Mr Hare. We need a clear head. This makes us a more stable partnership, Doctor. From Burke and Hare ta Knox, Burke and Hare, or Burke, Hare and Knox. Or even Burke, Knox and Hare. Whatever, it's got an honest ring about it.

HARE: Burke and Hare will honour the contract, written or not. You've ma word on it. We'll fill every corpse order because we know where them that's awa' will lie.

BURKE: That's what we were going ta tell you just now, Doctor. We're Scottish but Irish with it, dinnae ken the noo, begorra; and we have the gift of second sight with the third eye – here, here, in the middle of our heads. We can see by our third eye if a man or woman's marked doon ta die.

HARE: Ma grandmother, Martha O'Flynn, had the eye. An aura, leaky or whole. If the aura's dark and torn, that's bad. We meet a man or woman and with our third eye we can see a dark haze round their defective parts, throat, mouth, heart.

Those parts'll go and soon all of 'em's gone too.

BURKE: So we know who's going ta drop from the torn auras. That's how we get 'em so fresh. We've noted doon some new torn ones ready fer dropping: brisk Widow Dockery, Master Campbell, Ann McDougal, old beggarwoman McBride and her grandson, Mary Paterson's daughter, Daft Jamie. You'll soon be seeing.

DR KNOX: I only believe the evidence of ma two sound eyes. But I can understand you developing a special eye fer the dead, grubbing around graveyards, coffins, winding sheets and rotting flesh.

HARE: It's our living, Doctor.

DR KNOX: When can I have the carcass?

BURKE: Twa hours. We'll bring it over personal, Doctor, personal.

DR KNOX: Good . . . (*He puts down his glass.*) I'm already late for a number of appointments. Keep the corpses coming. It's vital work. Remember, in your humble way, you're serving science, saving lives. Without corpses we cannae experiment, cannae teach properly. It's why we have incompetent butchers masquerading as surgeons. Dr Logan broke a record yesterday and killed three men in one operation. He amputated a patient's leg and he died, cut his assistant's finger by mistake and he died from the infection and a watching student dropped dead from a heart attack. Unbelievable . . . We can only get better surgeons with better teaching. So keep the corpses coming. It's a service ta humanity. You're a member of the great fraternity of scientists. Thanks in part, ta yer dirty work, we'll know more about the human body and slowly but surely eliminate all the ills that humanity is heir to. One by one we'll defeat those scourges of mankind – smallpox, typhoid, diphtheria, yellow fever, and men and women will climb ta the bonny uplands of perfect health and be able, at last, ta die of nothing. Keep the corpses coming!

(DR KNOX *exits Up Stage Centre.*)

HARE: Inspiring.

BURKE: It makes it even better ta know yer killing ta save lives and make money.

HARE: Time we was moving braw Mary Paterson.

BURKE: Into the tea-chest with her.

(*They pick up the body and cross with it to the chest in the centre of the room.*)

Open the lid, Mr Hare . . .

(HARE *opens the lid of the chest.*)

In with her . . . In nomine patris . . .

(*They drop the body into the chest and shut the lid with a bang.*)

This is a great moment for us, Mr Hare; mark it. I know, whatever disappointments there may be in store, we'll look back on this moment as our very finest, when we were at our best, haloed.

HARE: Our disappointments'll be minor, Mr Burke. I smell oysters and champagne in the air. We're on the royal road ta success.

BURKE: Why's that, Mr Hare?

HARE: Because we're like lavender and lace . . .

BURKE: Time and tide . . .

HARE: Burke and Hare . . .

BURKE ⎫
HARE ⎭ : (*Singing*) 'Like meat and potatoes
Or salt and tomatoes
Boy what a blend
Don't put it in the papers
Don't leave it in the air
Don't keep it on the shelf
Put it there!'

(*They exit with the chest, laughing uproariously.*)

THE THREE VISIONS

Darkness. The sound of a door opening . . . a forest fire . . . a cricket match . . . a ship's foghorn . . . a gunshot . . . eggs frying . . . waves . . . Lights up on PETER BARNES, *sitting in Sound Studio B11, Broadcasting House, listening to sound effects. He clicks them off.*

BARNES: (*To himself*) It's the liar's world of sound . . . (*He switches on the sound effect of an aircraft.*) It could be a jet flying across the roof of the world . . . or Neasden. (*The sound of applause.*) A hundred men clapping . . . or one man overlaid a hundred times. (*The sound of a horse galloping.*) That's a horse in my head . . . not someone banging two empty coconut shells together. (*A woman is heard crying.*) Amid the alien corn they sit down to weep when they remember Zion . . . (*He clicks off the sound effects again as the door opens Stage Left and a young man enters.*) Can I help?

YOUNG MAN: I hope I'm not interrupting anything?

BARNES: No, I was just playing around with some sound effects. When the cat's away the mice do play. The production team's on a fifteen-minute coffee break. But can I help?

YOUNG MAN: Is this Studio B11?

BARNES: Broadcasting House, Portland Place, W1. Yes.

YOUNG MAN: Maybe I'm wrong. I thought I had to go to B11. Actually, I'm lost. It's my first visit here.

BARNES: It happened to me my first time, as well. Broadcasting House is a labyrinth. It's built on the same principle as the famous one in Crete. Thousands of doors and miles of circular corridors, round and round and round and round. You can only find your way out with the help of God or a uniformed guard. Some of the poor devils trapped in its passages and rooms go mad. I think the building's a visual symbol of poor ignorant man trapped in a labyrinth of culture.

YOUNG MAN: Excuse me but haven't we met somewhere?

BARNES: It's funny, I was thinking the same thing. Ever since you came in I've had this odd feeling we've met in similar circumstances . . . I'm recording a play of mine called *The Three Visions*. I'm Peter Barnes.

YOUNG MAN: But . . . my name's Peter Barnes, as well. The Writers' Guild never told me there was another Peter Barnes.

BARNES: You're a writer, too?

YOUNG MAN: Yes, I've come to discuss an idea of mine for a programme called *My Ben Jonson*.

BARNES: Your Ben Jonson?

YOUNG MAN: No, *My* Ben Jonson.

BARNES: But that's the name of a programme I wrote for the BBC years ago. Where do you live?

YOUNG MAN: Frampton Street.

BARNES: Frampton Street? Above the Chinese restaurant? On the corner?

YOUNG MAN: Yes.

BARNES: That's where I lived for years. A one-room flat. Top floor. Kitchen to the left, bathroom to the right as you come in. Glass animals on the window sill and bookshelves right underneath. I had a cloth-bound 1919 edition of the Webb's *History of Trade Unionism*, Fred Allen's *Treadmill to Oblivion* and . . .

YOUNG MAN: But I have those books, too. And the glass animals. What's going on? Where are we?

BARNES: Broadcasting House, May 20th, 1986.

YOUNG MAN: No, this is May 20th, 1962.

BARNES: No . . . 1986 . . . (*He hands him a newspaper.*) Here's the paper. Look at the date – 1986.

YOUNG MAN: I've got today's paper . . . (*He hands it to him.*) See, the date's 1962.

BARNES: They both can't be right.

YOUNG MAN: Just as both of us can't be Peter Barnes, can we?

BARNES: But don't you see how alike we are? Look in the mirror there. Same height, build, features – high forehead, weak chin, bleary eyes behind the glasses.

YOUNG MAN: Yes, the chin is weak, isn't it? I've never liked myself in profile.

BARNES: Terrible. Look, the only difference is I'm twenty-four years older. Despite the greying hair and paunch, I don't think I'm in too bad a shape for fifty-five.

YOUNG MAN: And I'm thirty-one . . . No, this is impossible! (*He sits down.*)

BARNES: I've found, over the years, the impossible happens more than you'd think possible.

YOUNG MAN: It's a dream. It must be a dream.

BARNES: I don't know about you but I don't dream much.

YOUNG MAN: Never. Well, almost never. I had one once. It's the only one I remember. I was being chased by a tiger over the edge of a precipice. I managed to cling to a vine high up the cliff-face. A mouse came out of its hole and started gnawing at the vine. Then I saw a strawberry growing nearby, so holding on to the vine with one hand, I picked the strawberry with the other and ate it. God how sweet it was. I can still taste it even though it was only a dream.

BARNES: I don't remember dreaming that. It sounds very literary. You probably read it somewhere. It's one of the reasons I never used dreams in my writing, they all sound so literary.

YOUNG MAN: True, and besides, the real world's dreamlike enough for me.

BARNES: And me. But this dream could be another exception, like the tiger, the mouse and the strawberry. What did I eat last night? Ah, Transylvanian stuffed cabbage and minced goose. But if this is a dream, who's dreaming who? Am I dreaming myself younger or are you dreaming yourself older?

YOUNG MAN: I think it's me dreaming older. But it's natural, if this meeting's a dream, each of us would believe he's the dreamer.

BARNES: If it is a dream.

YOUNG MAN: If it isn't and you really are me, how come you don't remember this meeting with a middle-aged man in B11, Broadcasting House in 1962, who told you he was Peter Barnes, too?

BARNES: Yes . . . I might've forgotten the incident because it was so bizarre. But that's not likely. You're probably right, it is a dream.

YOUNG MAN: So what do we do?

BARNES: Dream on.

YOUNG MAN: I've had a terrible thought . . . will we ever wake from it?

BARNES: One of us will. If it's your dream, you'll do better out of it than me. If it's mine, I just get to see me as I was. No point in me asking you questions, I'll know the answers. But you'll see me as you will be. So you can find out about my past which is your future. There must be things you want to know?

YOUNG MAN: Yes, so long as it doesn't get too personal. I don't want to hear who's alive, who's dead, who did what to me and what I did to them in my turn. I've never gone in for the strictly personal.

BARNES: You'll write, 'I've always seen the world of the strictly personal as shallow, tending to break life up into little closed cells. I have therefore tried, as far as possible, to keep any conscious autobiographical element out of my plays.'

YOUNG MAN: My dreams as well, it seems. I'm glad I'm going to write that.

(*The studio door opens and an* OLD MAN *comes in.*)

OLD MAN: This is B11, isn't it? I hope I'm not interrupting anything, *ahhhh.* (*He trips and goes sprawling across the studio, knocking against the tapedeck and inadvertently switching it on to the sound of seagulls cawing.* BARNES *and the* YOUNG MAN *rush over and pick up the* OLD MAN.) I'm all right.

(*They help him towards a chair.*)

YOUNG MAN: I'll switch off the sound.

BARNES: Good.

OLD MAN: I must've tripped. Hope I haven't damaged the equipment.

YOUNG MAN: (*Fiddling with the switch.*) I can't switch it off, it's jammed.

BARNES: Don't worry, just turn it down, if you can. The knob's on the right.

(*The sound of the seagulls continues quietly in the background.*)

OLD MAN: Sorry about all that but my plastic knee keeps conking out.

BARNES: You've got a plastic knee? I've got a plastic knee, too.

YOUNG MAN: You've got a plastic knee? I haven't got a plastic knee. How did you come to get a plastic knee?

BARNES: I fell off the stage when I was directing *Bartholomew Fair* at the Roundhouse Theatre back in '78. Don't worry, the surgeon promised the new knee would last longer than the rest of my body. He said that if they came to open up my coffin in the future, they'd find a pile of dust and one solitary plastic kneecap slightly mildewed, but still intact.

OLD MAN: But . . . that's how it happened to me . . . Exactly. Back in '78 I fell off the stage directing *Bartholomew Fair* at the Roundhouse Theatre – those imbeciles!

BARNES: You fell off, directing *Bartholomew Fair*?

YOUNG MAN: What's your name?

OLD MAN: Peter Barnes.

BARNES: The writer Peter Barnes?

OLD MAN: Where?! Where?!

BARNES: You!

OLD MAN: Oh yes, I'm the writer – *the* Peter Barnes.

YOUNG MAN: No, you're just *a* Peter Barnes. You see, I'm Peter Barnes, too.

BARNES: So am I. Peter Barnes aged fifty-five.

YOUNG MAN: Barnes aged thirty-one.

OLD MAN: Barnes aged seventy-four.

YOUNG MAN: We've decided, strictly between ourselves, it's a dream.

BARNES: I thought it was either me dreaming back or him dreaming forward. Now, with you here, it could be you dreaming back, him dreaming forward or me dreaming back or forward.

OLD MAN: Can you say that again?

BARNES: Not without spitting or loosening my teeth.

OLD MAN: But I don't dream much, except with my eyes open. It's one of the reasons I've never used dreams in my writing. Actually, I had one once, I seem to remember, about lions and raspberries.

BARNES: We've been through all that. If it isn't a dream, it means you'd remember when you were thirty-one meeting two idiots in Broadcasting House claiming they were you.

YOUNG MAN: And when you were fifty-five you'd have another meeting with two idiots claiming to be you in exactly the same place as before. Do you remember them?

OLD MAN: There are a lot of things I don't remember: old minds have problems. But I'm sure I'd've remembered that. I'm looking at you closely. Did I look like you then . . . when . . . ? Yes, those're the faces that stared back at me from the mirrors of my life. And I recognize my voice by the shape of the words. It's a dream most likely. And it's probably me dreaming it. If it is, I must know all about you – though nowadays, I've forgotten most of it – but you two certainly don't know about me.

BARNES: It's possible to dream the future as well as the past.

OLD MAN: Wait, I hope this isn't going to get personal! I've avoided it all my literary life. Leave that sort of thing to Americans. Only colossal personalities can be of benefit to society by drawing attention to their private lives. But that's not us. Not by a long chalk.

BARNES: We've been through all that, too. This is going to be strictly impersonal dreamstuff.

YOUNG MAN: I've just thought, if this isn't a dream, it could be a miracle.

OLD MAN: I prefer dreams. Miracles're too damn disturbing. Think of poor old Lazarus coming back from the dead,

graveyard stinking, just when his relatives were
divvying up his estate. And Jesus walking on the water like
a Jesus lizard. How many people drowned do you think,
when they tried it? Better steer clear of miracles.

BARNES: I don't know, it is something of a miracle if you're the
dreamer. I never thought I'd reach seventy-four. I was
certain the human race would've blown itself to pieces by
then.

OLD MAN: Perhaps they have and we're just the spirit of Peter
Barnes, floating in space – his aura, his energy.

BARNES: He never had much of either.

YOUNG MAN: Certainly not enough to be split three ways.
(*They laugh in agreement. The sound effect changes to the sound
of distant battle: the sound of clashing sword, pike and musket.*)
It's much easier to handle if it's a dream. So, you're me
later. How exactly do you feel, Mr Seventy-Four?

OLD MAN: Fine, Thirty-One. I've only fallen down once today.
I'm in pretty good shape, considering. Some men look as
wrinkled as last year's apples at my age. Of course, my
sight isn't too good. I keep losing things, like streets and
large buildings. And, of course, I've got a hernia,
rheumatism in my fingers and warts on the back of my
hands.

BARNES
YOUNG MAN } : (*Groaning*) Oh Lord.

OLD MAN: The other side, gentlemen, this is my deaf ear. I sit
on park benches a lot now. I've got asthma . . . I'm
overweight . . . and it's your fault. You two didn't take care
of me when you had the chance. Didn't listen. Too busy
writing and you eat too fast. Oh yes, and my shoulder
slopes at a twenty-degree angle. That's you two carrying a
heavy briefcase around all my life.

BARNES: Living in the city didn't help. But trees and fields
always made me feel dizzy.

OLD MAN: My mind's still as sharp as a billiard ball. Except on
bad days. Then, if anyone says 'hello', they have to wait
while I struggle for an answer.

(*The sound effect changes to the interior of a speeding train.*)

YOUNG MAN: So I deteriorated. That's expected. Built-in obsolescence of the total equipment. But what happened to the three-masted schooner of the soul? Do I still write hoping to make the world a little better?

OLD MAN: I remember saying something like that centuries ago. Sometimes I'm sorry for horses because they can't pick their noses but that's as far as I go now. At seventy-four and conscious, who hopes for 'better'?

BARNES: At fifty-five, the middle-watch has the worst of it, swinging between hope and no hope. It's hard. Nothing changes. Thanks to the poor, the rich and powerful are still with us, stealing freedom and everything else that isn't nailed down: freedom for the pike and barracuda is still death to the tadpole.

OLD MAN: Weep your hearts out and smile Jimmy Plato, Al Socrates and Harry Aristotle.

BARNES: But I still hope, hoping against hope. An artist must try to educate and raise himself above the moral climate of his audience.

OLD MAN: If you stood on a cigar box, you'd be above them. Appealing to the worst instincts of the public always pays well. That's why I'm broke and the wind whistles up my arse on Parliament Fields.

YOUNG MAN: Do I still write the way I've always tried writing, without compromise?

OLD MAN: Chicken scratches, chicken scratches, *cluck-cluck-cluck.*

BARNES: I'm still fool enough to believe in it. The plays get written, some even get on. I had a running success back in '69, mark the day. On one of my last opening nights, the curtain rose at 7.30, the audience at 7.40.

YOUNG MAN: So I still chain myself to the oars at the British Museum Reading Room?

BARNES: Odd, that's another circular structure. Yes, I'm still there or some other public venue, doing my time. Grey days without it. See, these are the calloused hands of poetry.

OLD MAN: I can tell you, I've conceded the race to the
quick and hung my hat in the hall. Well, almost. The
habits of a lifetime're difficult to break. I sit on park
benches, blow on my fingers, put on my woolly mittens and
scratch, scratch, scratch out a few little lyrics when the
mood's on me and the Scotsmen in hobnail boots tap dance
through my mind. No epics now, Ginger, not wanted on
voyage. I've narrowed down to light verses for music no
longer written. Silent songs. The latest one's called 'Yank
My Doodle, It's a Dandy'.

YOUNG MAN: Yank My Doodle . . . ?!

OLD MAN: I'm sorry, I'm too old for that sort of thing now!

BARNES: You know – but of course you would, wouldn't you – I
started writing lyrics a couple of years ago. There's a ballad
going around in my head now.

OLD MAN: Is it the one about the Irishman who broke both his
ankles making coconut wine?

BARNES: No, it's about my knee, my knee.

OLD MAN: (*Singing*) 'My knee, my knee
My very special knee
It used to work quite perfectly
But then I smashed it accidentally.'

BARNES: (*Singing*) 'And now I have a plastic knee
My knee, my knee.
They won't remember me,
Just my knee, my knee.'

OLD MAN: (*Singing*) 'Ah me, ah me.'

YOUNG MAN: I just don't understand you two. We're too
similar and too different. We're caricatures of each other.

OLD MAN: All chicken scratches, chicken scratches,
cluck-cluck-cluck. Did you know, only chickens can
unscramble eggs by eating them?

BARNES: That's the kind of gratuitous information I'm always
coming out with.

YOUNG MAN: One more question. What about recognition? Will
I get any?

BARNES: Now it comes, the worm in the bud, ambition, the

desire for fame and glory.

(*The sound of a desert wind.*)

OLD MAN: There's no need to feel awkward about it, Thirty-One. Amateurs are the only people who do things without the desire for fame or money or the hope of ever doing it well. And you, him, me, we've never been that, not never, ever.

BARNES: As for recognition, zilch, zero, the fat 'o'. Sorry. A collected edition of the plays and an independent study of them, is about the size of it. How about you, Seventy-Four? Are you the Dirty Old Man of English Letters, OBE, CBE, MCC?

OLD MAN: I'm a BF. But I've always been that. Face it, Thirty-One, you've risen from obscurity and are headed for oblivion. When you die, there'll be no two-minute silence along Shaftesbury Avenue or Broadway, and Bloom's and Lindy's won't serve black matzo balls as a mark of respect.

BARNES: You had a tale to tell and you passed like passing water.

YOUNG MAN: My life doesn't sound as if it's going to be a barrel of laughs.

OLD MAN: The bum wants to be happy!

BARNES: Lad, some writers are born with silver spoons in their mouths – not even their agents can stop them being successful. That isn't you, me, him or even us.

YOUNG MAN: But I want to be happy and rich and great and uncompromising and revolutionary and famous.

BARNES: You're a stranger to me now but at this very moment I feel close to you, Thirty-One.

YOUNG MAN: Why should trees be happy and rocks and sticks of celery and even old boots and not me?

OLD MAN: It's the Northern light and the old Puritan belief of literary excellence through personal misery. I smile and rub my hands together but nobody's fooled.

YOUNG MAN: I have to say it, gentlemen, I'm disappointed in you two.

BARNES: You have to share the blame. You were too proud.

Everything is approximate but I wanted perfection. What arrogance! Why struggle for precision and purity, when they can never be attained?

YOUNG MAN: You struggle because it's right.

OLD MAN: You were too passionate. I never played it smooth, like Guzzler's Gin, s-m-o-o-t-h, s-m-o-o-t-h.

YOUNG MAN: Smooth! You should've chewed them up and spat out their buttons!

OLD MAN: 'The roads get longer and my legs shorter and I take smaller steps every day.' You'll write that.

YOUNG MAN: Don't keep quoting me, it's depressing.

(*The sound of a single heartbeat.*)

BARNES: Yes, it is, with you sitting there like a visible conscience.

YOUNG MAN: Tell me, what did I do?

BARNES: Very little.

YOUNG MAN: What did I achieve?

OLD MAN: Nothing . . . That gives my heart a deeper wound than death.

BARNES: A good line. I may use it.

OLD MAN: You will, Oscar, you will.

YOUNG MAN: I'm sick of you and I'm sick of him and I'm sick of me. I'm a sick man. But I'm still going to follow my vision. You can betray me but you won't stop me!

BARNES: It's no good you shouting, just as it's no good us giving you advice. You're going to become the persons we are. But you can help us.

OLD MAN: How can that bespectacled prig I was, help me? Oh, and I always thought I was such a social and easygoing sort of *bon vivant* when I was young. He's about as *bon vivant* as a cactus. There's no consolation backwards, memory is fear. I sit on my park benches and dream what's left of my life away. That's what I'm doing now. I'm slipping off the edge of the world . . . down and then the darkness.

BARNES: I feel it, too, but he can help us.

OLD MAN: Can he tell me if I'm going to have an easy death? That's all I want to know.

BARNES: He can at least tell us why we started in the profession, on the game – writing.

OLD MAN: I didn't know any better, *cluck-cluck-cluck*.

YOUNG MAN: I write to discover the truth about life, to be in the vanguard of the struggle for the happiness of all mankind, to rouse the dead to get up and fight.

OLD MAN: Was that why?

BARNES: Yes, I remember.

OLD MAN: I thought it was to keep me off the streets.

BARNES: I slid into it like a dream.

(*The sound effect of a match being struck, a fuse being lit and someone running away.*)

OLD MAN: At times my body used to be able to fly . . .

BARNES: And my mind grasp the true nature of the universe . . .

(*There is the sound of a bomb exploding. Then silence.*)

YOUNG MAN: Is that it?

BARNES: It should be.

OLD MAN: It doesn't sound like it, we're still talking.

BARNES: Maybe we're just dead and in Purgatory: stuck in the BBC for all eternity.

YOUNG MAN: We must've done something really bad.

OLD MAN: More likely something we didn't do.

BARNES: Shhh.

(*There is the sound of distant footsteps. They come nearer.*)

BARNES: It's the production team coming back.

OLD MAN: Or another sound effect. Let's go out on an up note. The knee song.

YOUNG MAN
BARNES   } : (*Singing*) 'Oh my knee, my knee
OLD MAN   They won't remember me
                  Just my knee, my knee'.

(*They laugh as the lights fade down and the footsteps are louder now.*)

YOUNG MAN: Someone wake up . . . please.

(*The sound of the studio door opening in the darkness.*)

NOTES

Writing, not so much an expression of subjectivity but a search for new knowledge, new ways of seeing.

Writing which has a moral purpose in the service of politics; not politics as propaganda but, rather, teaching by example.

Writing in which reality's concreteness is worked on, but not dissolved by making it abstract or butchered to fit some preconceived ideology. For that which lives by subject matter alone, quickly dies with it.

Writing to convey a knowledge which is not empirical information which the author possesses but judgement which he or she has gained by writing; a judgement which perhaps provides within itself the capacity for action, if not immediately, then later.

Ultimate complexity of thought and language with absolute clarity of expression.

The fear that might hold me back from going too far in a sentence is only another example of unconscious control and therefore artistic stupefaction.

A drama of extremes, trying to illuminate the truth as contradictory. Instead of eliminating those contradictions as untrue, they are emphasized; melancholy and joy, tragedy and comedy, the bathetic and the sublime are placed side by side. The similarity of such opposites is shown by such juxtapositions. What we call tragic or comic are, in fact, their opposites, for it is a principle of dialectical logic that what seems on the surface one thing, is essentially its opposite. So incompatible and widely contradictory elements are superimposed on each other till they are transformed into reality, which is itself made up of similar contradictory elements also existing side by side with each other.

Quotations taken out of their original context mean something different, placed in a different setting. This is one way to discover the new within the old.

To scrutinize certain concrete and conceptless details of life in such a way as to show their transcendental meaning, without for once leaving the empirical living world or forgetting the facts of life.

The value of art, which is other than given reality, must depend on how fitting the artistic form is to the content or idea which it expresses.

Why is there always a gap between the words and the things they conjure up?

A play has to be translated from the written text into sounds and movements, which means it has to be thought through and interpreted in order to exist. In the reproduction of a drama on stage, two moments of creation and interpretation exist simultaneously.

Theatre should be a passion for knowledge.

Writers in the process of imitating brute matter transform it so that it can now be read as an expression of social truth.

Questions:

(1) What to do with audiences who know what they want because they think they know what other people want?

(2) What can a writer do when confronted with human beings incapable of believing or sympathizing with anything they have not experienced?

(3) Do the correct political tendency and correct artistic tendency converge? Is the purpose to produce valid art or to change society? This is not a question because they are, of course, the same thing. However, if the artistic technique is at fault, does it mean that the revolutionary message is invalid? Does the purity of the artistic technique in itself correspond to its revolutionary message? In fact, is truth not just *what* is said but *how*?